ONE MAN'S WAR

STEVEN SAVILE

AETHON
BOOKS

ONE MAN'S WAR

Print and eBook formatting, and cover design by Steve Beaulieu.

Published by Aethon Books LLC.

PROLOGUE

There is no good way to prepare yourself to die.

But that's what we did every time we took on a gig. We made peace with the fact that there's every chance one of the crew wouldn't make it out. That's one of the reasons they paid us the big bucks. Randall Fate is the other one. Or was the other one. It was hard to think of him being gone, especially because of some stupid, stupid mistake. If he wasn't already dead, I'd kill him. Seriously. He shouldn't have been making rookie mistakes. He wasn't some wet behind the ears kid. He was the best of us. Him dying was like a punch in the dick.

It had all started to unravel when the four of us went into Africa to hit Akachi Corp for GenX. It was supposed to be a simple in-and-out, no hanging around. Minimal risk. Fate had done the recce and had it all worked out. We trusted him. He was the man with the plan.

Now he's the man in the box they're shoveling dirt onto.

It's not exactly a poetic end, but live by violence, die by violence. It's the only way.

I'd promised myself I wasn't going to come. I really didn't want to. I was done with him long before the gig went south. He was bad news. That's why I went for the compromise. I could see the graveside but wasn't there with Martagan and Swann pretending to be broken-hearted. I lurked beneath a weeping willow, off in the shadows of the crematorium's furnace. They couldn't see me. As far as they were concerned, I'd flaked and was out of my mind in one of the district's Beetle dens. I've always figured it got the name Beetle because it makes your skin crawl on the comedown. In truth, they wouldn't have been far off. I wasn't in a good place and hadn't been since before Africa. I'd been looking for a way out. That's the thing about this life, the bigger the job, the more money it paid and the greater the likelihood of failure. Our crew had a good reputation. We'd done some profile jobs. No one wanted to go up against us. But that becomes a problem, too. You never want to be the best gunslinger in town. When you are, all the young punks come looking to take you down, but that's how reputations are made. It was no different when we were starting out. Fate identified the kind of crews we wanted to go up against to make our name, then made sure we tendered for the right jobs.

It should have been raining.

It was supposed to rain at these things.

It wasn't supposed to be bright sunlight.

Sweat crept down the back of my neck and gathered at the base of my spine, sticky and uncomfortable.

I'd never realized the old man was religious, but they gave him a proper send-off, black-clad priest, prayers and promises of the afterlife and all. Ashes, ashes, we all fall down, eventually. Martagan stooped over the hole in the ground and tossed a handful of dirt inside. Whatever she said didn't carry to my hiding place. I knew I should just go over there, make my peace with everyone and move on, but I never got the chance.

The first gunshot rang out.

For a moment Martagan seemed to teeter on the edge of the open grave, then whatever threads held her to this life were severed, and she went down.

They came out of the shadows. Four men. They moved fast, with military precision. They broke right and left, dividing Swann's focus. Not that he could've done anything. The second shot took him in the knee. He clutched at the shattered joint, screaming. There's nothing in the world like the sound of a gunshot. It sends a cold chill right to the listener's core with a promise of what that *crack* is delivering. Four more shots came in quick succession, their reports echoing around the canyon of the cemetery and out, hitting the high glass walls of the skyscrapers overlooking the bone garden. His body jerked and twisted, kept up momentarily by the bullets. A single shot to the left shoulder turned him one way, one in his right jerked him back the other way a split-second later another to the gut doubled him up for the coup de grâce, a headshot, put him down.

I couldn't move.

I wanted to.

Honestly.

But I couldn't.

It wouldn't have made any difference if I had, that was the grim reality of it, so I stood there, still half-hidden by shadows, and watched my friends die. I felt sick. I had to get out of there, but before I could, I made a second hit squad, meaning eight men had been sent to take us out. It was flattering in a way. There were only three of us. With surprise, they should have ended us in five seconds flat. Making their move as Martagan said her goodbyes was smart. She never saw it coming, and Swann didn't have time to react. They had a sniper up on the rooftop of the lowest building overlooking the cemetery covering the one gate into the place. Another spotter had taken up position behind one of the mausoleums. The light reflected off his rifle's sight. It was a rookie mistake. That just made the fact that his bullet was the one that took out Martagan all the more insulting. It's one thing to die at the hands of a stone-cold killer, it's another to be taken out by an amateur. She'd have absolutely hated that.

They had all the angles covered. If I'd tried to do something, they would have cut me down before I'd made it halfway across the graveyard. And I couldn't leave. All I could do was watch as one of them stood over Swann, placed the barrel of their gun against his forehead and delivered a double-tap, opening up a baseball-sized hole in the back of his skull. They weren't taking any chances. His body twitched for a couple of seconds, and then that was that. My entire crew wiped out in the time it took to say 'forgive me, father, for I have sinned.' Not that I was in the mood for confessing anything.

That was when I realized they'd never have made their move if they didn't know I was in there.

I looked down and saw the red dot in the middle of my chest.

PART ONE

TEMPTING FATE

Fate played his hand.

The first card he laid down was the family one. I knew it was coming. He was like a broken record.

"Come on, Guerra, we're brothers. We're in this together."

"Don't say all for one or any of that crap, Randall."

"The money's good," he said.

"The money was good last time. Ask me if that makes the colossal screw-up any easier to take. Go on, ask me."

Fate shook his head. "I don't need to. I get it. I do. But I'm asking you to trust me. Can you do that? Can you trust me?"

"No." Honest and to the point. I've never been big on bullshit. It wastes a lot of time. The stunt he'd pulled in Rio had angered a lot of people. That, by itself, wouldn't have been so bad, but he'd committed one of the cardinal sins: he'd got wind of a gig going down in the city and put us between the contractors hired by the corporation to do the job and their prize, effectively poaching the gig and then holding the corp to ransom. Not big. Not clever.

We were in Fate's place on the thirty-second floor of the Wan Chai plaza with a view of the sky church across the square. No one was looking out through the windows. There were fifty-two floors above us and a communications mast that could have tickled the Divine's ballsack if he bent over. We are talking prime real estate. Fate picked the place up at north of thirty million, one for each floor.

Lisl Martagan wasn't watching. She only had eyes for the monarch butterfly that had somehow gotten loose in the atrium and was fluttering from place to place, never landing for long. She tracked it across the room, watching its shadow flit across the wall, before anticipating where it would land next and splitting it in two with a deft backhanded flick of the wrist that sent a small silver star on its lethal trajectory. I knew better than to expect the butterfly to fly off. Martagan didn't miss. Ever. She didn't see me looking at her. She looked good, not sexy, not pretty, just good. Dangerous. Martagan wore her silver-white hair close-cropped, the fringe feathered across her forehead, accentuating her sharp features and sharper nose. She looked like a woman you wouldn't want to meet in a dark alley.

"Think about it," she said, not looking at me. "You owe it to him, Marco."

She always called me Marco, not Guerra. We'd had a thing once, back in New Delhi. It had been her doing. So had ending it. She stopped short of calling it a mistake, but it was the kind of mistake I'd happily have made a second time.

Swann put his ZEK-39 on the glass table and spun it with his index finger, halfway between a game of spin the bottle and Russian roulette. "I'm with Guerra. I don't care what anyone says, it's hot out there. We should wait 'til it cools down a bit."

He wasn't talking about the weather.

"He's got a point," I said. "The smart thing to do would be to lie low for a while. There're a lot of people out there who aren't very happy with us. People who happen to have an awful lot of money and aren't used to having things not go their way." There were a few too many negatives in that sentence, but everyone knew what I meant.

"We can handle whatever they throw at us," Fate assured me.

And he genuinely believed that.

"That's not the point," I said. "We shouldn't have to. If we're taking a job, we need to be one hundred percent focused on it, not sleeping with one eye open or looking back over our shoulders as we go in. That's how mistakes get made. I'm not happy about this."

"Duly noted," Fate said. "But it's a good job. It's simple. And they're willing to pay top dollar because it's us. Because we *are* that good."

They call people like us Bleeders. We bleed for our corporate paymasters, literally, not in some sort of glorified romantic sense of loyalty. It's an insult, not a term of endearment, but we've laid claim to it. I'll happily call myself a Bleeder, after all, we're paid to be shot at and cut up, fragged and generally battered until we're shitting blood. It's not exactly pretty. Because of that, reputations count for a lot in this game. You're only as good as your last gig. Ours had been an utter bollocks job, to be honest, but we'd still got it done which is more than a lot of crews might have done. We've got a saying in this game: any gig you can walk away from is a good gig. That's pushing it a bit, but for anyone keeping score that meant we were batting forty-nine not out. From the outside looking in we were that good. You didn't last long if you weren't. It wasn't just about fancy apartments and fast cars. Sometimes something as simple as staying alive was a good way of measuring a crew's success.

"Talk me through it," I said. "But I'm not making any promises."

"The job's in Africa. It's a simple in-and-out, no hanging around. GenX are offering us double our usual fee because they want the best, and in case you haven't noticed, that's us, my grumpy friend. They've got us covered for a drop ship into Akachi Corp territory. Our target's a lab where they've been developing some sort of hybrid chip. Our guy at GenX wants it because he thinks he can reverse engineer the tech to use in some new process they've been developing to overwrite personalities for the Justice Department. Ours is not to wonder why."

I didn't like the sound of that. Overwriting personalities? Sure, I could see the argument for protecting the populace and ordinary decent people having nothing to fear, but the reality was a handful of corporations ruled the world, not governments, not royalty, and their only loyalty is to the shareholders. Piss off the wrong corporate master, and they schedule you for a rewrite? No thank you. The world's going in directions I don't like. There's the augmentation brigade, the transhumans who believe they're more machine than man and visit back-street chop shops of illegal operations to switch out pesky human parts for robotic replacements. There's a brisk trade in body parts. Call me old fashioned, but I kinda like the idea of being the only one who can get inside my head and see what I'm really thinking. We're not talking PG-13 thoughts most of the time, for starters. Giving the corporations access to my innermost fetishes and those dark midnight thoughts where I dream about settling a few old scores with a good old oxy-acetylene torch? Hell no. I'd be first in line for a rewrite.

"We'll need to breach their security, which is where Swann comes in," he offered a self-deprecating smile. "Then once we're inside it's a case of locating the biochem labs and finding the prototype chip, then we make like shepherds and get the flock out of there."

"You make it sound easy," I said, wryly.

I should have known better.

Nothing in this life is easy.

We made the rendezvous point at oh six hundred hours. The transport was waiting for us on the hard stand. An Anaconda X-11, about forty thousand kilos of steel, vertical take-off thrusters, capable of low earth orbit. It was more than just a plane. It was a flying fortress. "I see we're going for the element of surprise," I joked.

Fate scratched that little patch of skin behind his ear. He did that when he was nervous—meaning he'd been holding something back. Looking at the Anaconda's cargo bay doors, I had a sinking feeling.

"Is there something you want to tell me?"

"We're good."

"I'm not entirely sure we are."

"No. We are. You have my word." He might as well have said he had diamond mine he wanted to sell me. I knew when he was spinning.

Swann came wandering over. He moved well for a man with a broken back. That was because of the exospine he was wearing. It was like a giant millipede that had anchored itself on his back, teeth sunk into the base of his neck, tapping into the brain stem. He controlled it with his mind. No one would guess he'd been paraplegic for fifteen years, his spine unilaterally severed between the T8 and T9 vertebrae. The exospine dispensed carefully regulated pain meds, too. He owed his life to tech developed by GenX in Brazil, meaning he owed his life to GenX. We never talked about what happened. I knew it was my fault. He knew it was my fault. We'd long since made peace with it.

I saw the spare chute in his hand, his own already on his back.

Thermal goggles hung around his neck. He had his ZEK-39 strapped to his thigh and a G1 Jackal assault rifle to complete the ensemble. Very much the chosen look for the mercenary about town in the 22nd Century. The scary thing was even with the frag grenades I knew he was packing it wasn't overkill. We were going to need all the firepower we could muster no matter what Fate reckoned.

"Please tell me we're not jumping out of that thing?"

Fate smiled at me.

The bastard.

"Don't think of it as jumping so much as hurtling toward the ground if that helps?"

Swann laughed. He was enjoying himself. He knew I wasn't good with heights.

I shook my head. "That's the point. We're talking about four maybe five minutes completely exposed up there. It's a long way down, and we'll be sitting ducks."

"Oh, yea of little faith, Marco," Fate said, still grinning. He held out his hand like a magician doing a reveal. In the middle of his palm was a small black puck with a small pressure plate in the center. A cloaking pack. "We free-fall for sixty seconds, then trigger this bad boy when we deploy the parachutes. No one will see us coming."

I didn't want to point out the obvious flaw in his plan, but I felt obligated to. "You do know that those things don't negate our thermal signature, right? And even if they shield us from the naked eye, they won't make us invisible to the equipment and sensors Akachi will have watching the skies."

"It'll do what we need it to do, besides we're not dropping right on top of them," Fate said, stubbornly. I was seriously getting fed up with his pig-headedness these days. He was starting to believe his own press. Always a mistake. How many death certificates should have had hubris written on them as the cause of death? I was seconds from walking away. I really should have. You get a sense for when jobs are bad. We're not talking flashing lights and sirens. It's subtler than that. But when you've been around the block as many times as I have, you can just tell when something's rotten. It's got its own unique stench. And this, this reeked.

But I got on that plane because we were a team.

Still.

Just.

We buckled up.

Long gone are the days of that thundering charge along the runway to get airborne. Now the pilot simply sets the vertical thrusters to take-off, and it's like going up in a great glass elevator. There are a couple of gut-wrenching seconds when the buildings of the city lurch away beneath you, then it's only sky, up and up, a cacophony fit to raise the dead never mind forty thousand kilos of steel. Up, up and away.

We didn't talk.

Martagan took the opportunity to grab a couple of hours' shut-eye. I always envied her ability to sleep anywhere. I was too keyed up to sleep. I'd got it into my head that we were headed for a metaphorical as well as physical fall. Swann tapped out an annoying one-note tune on the metal buckle of his harness. I'm sure that in his head it sounded like *Ride of the Valkyrie*, but in reality, it came across as a piss-poor attempt at Morse Code. Randall Fate was the least calm of us. He fidgeted in his bucket seat, itching to get moving.

Something was going on here.

Fate was never nervous.

The guy was the epitome of the calm, cold-blood, ruthless killer for hire.

He knew something we didn't.

I didn't like it.

"What aren't you telling us?" I asked, bluntly.

He looked at me like I'd just slapped him with my dick. He didn't meet my eyes. He looked out through the cargo bay doors to the ant-sized city below. Evasive. The world streaked by beneath us. We'd make Africa in two hours, less if the pilot took us all the way up into low orbit. It was no time at all.

"I asked you a question, Fate. There's something you're not telling us."

"You're right," he said, finally. I waited for him to expand on his confession. We must have covered twenty or thirty klicks before he did. "There's a chance—only a chance—that we might not be the only team down there."

"You've got us poaching another gig?" I couldn't quite believe what I was hearing. "Didn't we get into enough shit the last time?"

He shook his head. "It's not like that."

"Then what *is* it like?"

"This is our gig. The other team isn't after the chip."

"Right. So what *are* they after?"

"Me."

"You what?"

"Barnes put a price on my head after the last job. It's a lot of money. More than I'm worth, and you know I don't say that lightly. I think I dented his pride. Now there's a crew looking to collect."

"So, let me get this straight, we're going in to Akachi looking to steal their prize tech out from under their noses while another team's chasing us hell-bent on taking you out? Fan-*fucking*-tastic, Randall. And you didn't think to mention this before we were in the air because?"

"It doesn't change anything."

"Of course it changes things."

"It really doesn't. Break it down, the mission objectives haven't changed, all we're talking about is four more guns pointing our way."

"You really are a prick, Randall, you know that?"

"But you love me, Marco," he said, offering that rakish smile of his. He'd spent a lot of money on that smile. None of his teeth were real. It was all about image. Fate cared how people perceived him. I didn't. I never had. I cared about staying alive. I was happy for people to misjudge me. The more they underestimate me, the happier I am.

"Once upon a time, maybe, but I'm done. If we get out of this alive, I never want to hear from you again."

"Let's just worry about one thing at a time," Swann said, ever practical. He stopped tapping out his secret message. The sounds coming from the engines changed, deepening. We'd hit altitude. I thought very seriously about throwing Fate out through the cargo bay doors and seeing how quickly evolution would kick in and grant him wings. "You can be all noble and indignant when we're out of there, Marco. Right now, it's not helping."

"Listen to the man," Fate said as if Swann's wisdom was irrefutable.

"I'm not going to forget this," I said. They were the last words any of us said before we jumped.

⌖

The ground rushed toward me.

I counted out sixty-three seconds, the gee's contorting my face as I fell to earth. The wind battered me with the physical force of a herd of stampeding rhinos. Then on sixty-four I deployed the chute and hit the pressure plate on the cloaking pack, praying both would work. For about three seconds there I was devoutly religious, then I was back to being my good old atheistic self as the arrested momentum of the fall dragged me back up several hundred meters as the parachute opened.

Martagan was first out of the plane and already about a thousand meters below me, steering herself toward the landing zone.

There was no x marks the spot.

We couldn't jump too close to the Akachi Corp labs; they'd have all sorts of protection in place. The corporations were big on keeping their secrets. They paid top dollar to make sure they didn't leak. You couldn't expect to parachute in, land on a conveniently flat rooftop, blow a hole in the roof access door, storm the stairs to the lab a couple of floors down and walk out the front door with something they'd spent billions designing. Even Fate wasn't that stupid.

We were fifty klicks from the Akachi facility.

It didn't appear on any maps.

Hell, we only had Fate's word to go on that it even existed.

Fifty klicks was a safe distance, theoretically. But it meant we had serious ground to cover once we made landfall. The drop site was bleached bone-white by the incessant hammering of the sun. It made the glass and steel construction work on the other side of the ghettos stand out like a rash of black tumors. There was a manmade lake two klicks from the main site, with thick forestation around it. That was our target. Between us and the target a sprawling shanty town that had grown and grown until it was more than twenty klicks end-to-end. Even from above the poverty was painfully obvious, as were the missing rooftops on most of the dwellings. The aim was to come down close to the sprawl and pick up quad bikes that Fate had bought and paid for through a fixer back home. According to our intel, there was a manmade lake close to the Akachi facility, with underwater access to the main site via sewerage tunnels. I didn't fancy swimming two klicks through crap, but it was better than the alternative, being a sitting duck out on the open plains. We'd got breathing apparatus in our kit that just clipped on the nose and meant we could breathe for a good hour, hour and a half, without needing to open our mouths. I didn't ask where Fate had got his intel. I assumed he'd been drip fed it by his contact at GenX, meaning it was good but incomplete. That was how we had to work most of the time. We didn't exactly go in blind, but we hardly ever saw the whole picture.

We came down hard, hitting the dirt and rolling. First things first, we needed to ditch the chutes. We couldn't risk them being found and someone putting two-and-two together. I bundled my chute up, looking around for somewhere to bury it. The ground was hard-packed dirt and bedrock. There was no way I was going to get away with scooping up a few handfuls of dust and shoving the chute down into the shallow hole. "How long has that cloaking pack got left on the charge?"

"Long enough," Fate said, liking the way I was thinking.

We gathered the four parachutes together, making a nest out of them, and nestled the cloaking device in the center of the pile, then stepped away. Outside the narrow circumference of the force field, I couldn't see the chutes. It would have to do. The sun would be up in a couple of hours. It was already tortuously hot, the air thick and unbreathable with the stench of humanity drifting off the sprawling ghetto. Fate had coordinates for the rendezvous point where we were supposed to pick up the quads. We'd come down close to five klicks away from it. That meant running in the heat that was only going to get fiercer the longer we waited.

He gave the signal for us to move out.

Breathing hard, sweat dripping down the back of my neck, I was the first to reach the edge of the world.

The shanty town rose up in all of its squalid grandeur ahead of us. It was weird how what had obviously been temporary had become permanent. Homes that had never been finished now housed their third and fourth generation of poor. Rats scurried ahead, keeping to the shadows along the sides of the shanties. There was no running water in these places; central wells had been sunk down to the water table, standpipes offering the only water for miles around. That gave the place its own special stench, too. It was far too human.

"Two streets over," Fate said, checking our position against the global positioning satellite.

Kids, all slack skin and bone, were already out in the streets. A pair came toward us, hands cupped, begging. I shook my head. That didn't stop them. One of the boys was stupid enough to get too close to Martagan. She cuffed him around the ear and sent him scurrying off back toward the safety of the anonymous buildings. I heard voices. Raised. Angry. The kid came out again, hands cupped, obviously sent back out to face us and not come back without something to show for it.

They trailed in our wake, following us through the stinking streets until we reached the lock-up where Fate's fixer had sorted out our transport. Everything is for sale, especially in places where they can't afford to eat half the time. Most of the guys around here were skimmers. They scavenged waste from the Akachi facility and repurposed it for a profit. Everything that wasn't broken could find a new life, even stuff that was broken could be turned into something else by a creative skimmer if he put his mind to it. Evidence of that was all around us. We were walking through streets that were living proof of the skimmers inventiveness. A guy in tribal costume shuffled out of the door, waiting for Fate to cross his palm with silver. "Mabeziela?"

The chieftain nodded. "You are late," he said in broken English. "I had almost given up on you."

"We're here now. Are the quads fueled and ready?"

"As agreed."

"Good. We were never here."

"Of course," the chieftain nodded, opening the door wider and ushering us inside.

The quads were hidden under grubby tarpaulins. Fate pulled back one of the covers to inspect the bike. It wasn't what I expected. Yes, it had four wheels. Yes, it would probably cope with the terrain. But it appeared to be the bastard child of ten different write-offs from a chop shop welded together, all rusted plates and scavenged parts. "It works?" Fate asked.

"What do you take me for?" the tribesman countered, reaching down for the throttle and yanking on it to gun the engine. The quad spluttered a couple of times before the engine caught, but then it roared to life as he twisted the throttle a couple of times.

Satisfied, Fate followed the tribesman into the backroom to conclude their business.

The muffled report of the gunshot, the muzzle pressed up against the man's temple, meant they'd come to an arrangement about silence that wasn't exactly mutually beneficial. We had to move fast. We stripped the tarps and mounted up, gunning the engines. Fate hid the chieftain's body under one of the tarps.

We left dust and a dead man trailing behind us.

The shanty town was already beginning to wake up. The roar of the quad's engines didn't do us any favors. They were hellishly loud in the pre-dawn quiet. The good thing was that the locals associated the noise with raiders so didn't come looking to see what the noise was all about. That was part of our disguise. In order to really sell it, Fate guided us back through the streets and out into the desert region rather than through the streets of the shanty towns' sprawl. We were going around the outside, like desert raiders would. It was faster than trying to traverse the clogged streets of the makeshift city overflowing with festering garbage and the detritus of life. The place was a warren of hardship and hunger, growing more and more desperate the closer to the center you grew. If someone thought we were worth it, they'd sell the little knowledge they had. That made the whole in-and-out gig so much harder. Especially with another crew hunting us. The quads could handle the worst of the terrain, the broken rocks and cracked paths and everything else the land threw at them. The heat and suffocating air would be worse. And the higher the sun rose, the more grueling they would become. It was all about speed now.

We rode into the sunrise.

There was a forested region two klicks from the lake.

That's where we ditched the quads. The sun was still a couple of hours from being overhead. Ideally, we'd have gone in at night, but beggars couldn't be choosers. The obsidian glass of the Akachi lab was a marked contrast to the poverty we'd left behind. It screamed Big Money. The only thing it was lacking was the big corporate logo slapped across the huge dome that caught and reflected the sun like a prism across the desert. Both the lake and forest were manmade, meant to drive home just how rich the men behind this secret lab were. I got the point. It was hard not to.

We didn't need to talk. We understood each other. We'd been to hell and back. When you'd done that a few times you didn't need words. You just knew what the other person was doing and acted accordingly.

We pushed the quads into the trees.

Swann had the kit bag. Everything we'd need to breach Akachi's security. I took the breathing apparatus from him, clipped it in place over my nose, and plunged into the water, sinking in over my head. It was a sheer drop with concrete banks around us more like a huge swimming pool than a lake with a gently sloping shore. Ten feet under, it was darker but clear, the water around me rippling with a blue-green tinge. I breathed out a slow stream of bubbles, hoping they'd be drawn toward the pipe if the lake was servicing the facility, then kicked off, swimming toward the far shore.

The others followed.

It took a couple of minutes to find the eddies that in turn led to the drain, and beyond an iron grate, the pipeline that led into the heart of the facility. Swann moved to the front, placing a controlled c4 charge on the grate then swam back a safe distance before triggering the remote detonator. The explosion was almost silent, muffled by the incredible press of the water, but that only made the shockwave more pronounced, rippling out toward us like a great invisible fist. The sheer force of the blow hit hard, driving us back as we kicked and struggled not to be swept back into the high concrete banks behind us, and then echo of it was bullying us toward the opening and the twisted metal where the grate had been torn from its foundations by the explosives.

I swam through the opening, careful not to snag myself on the spears of metal.

The light went out within two powerful breaststrokes as the others entered the pipe behind me.

I triggered the glo-light built into my suit, turning the claustrophobic pipeline a sickly shade of green, and kept on swimming. Behind me, the others did the same.

I hate water.

Have I mentioned that?

I've never been the strongest swimmer, and two klicks in a pipe too narrow to properly finish any of the strokes made it all the more uncomfortable. It was claustrophobic. Air bubbles steamed up in front of my face. There were no air pockets above me. I was all too aware that my breathable air was running out, even if there was an hour or so left. We were swimming into the unknown, no matter

Fate's assurances. We had no idea what was waiting at the other end of the pipe. After about ten minutes I was pawing along the sides of the pipe, using it to propel me forward and relying on small kicks to keep me moving. I didn't trust Randall Fate. I wouldn't have led it past him to have sold us out to save his own skin. It was all about the money with him at the best of times. These weren't the best. My breath metallic in my throat, I pushed off the wall again. There was nothing to say that we weren't swimming toward a whole host of bullets. They wouldn't do a lot for my buoyancy.

There was a change in the quality of light up ahead.

The end of the pipe.

That, or I was about twenty meters from the afterlife.

I pushed on, my shoulders burning from the effort. There was a second iron grille between us and the light. We wouldn't be able to use c4 this time, the vibrations from the charge would set off pressure sensitive alarms and bring Akachi's security forces running. I motioned Swann forward, trying to make myself small so he could squeeze by above me. He had a high-intensity arc burner in his hand. The beam of the burner was no more than ten centimeters, but the heat it generated would cut through sheet steel like butter. The iron rebar was tougher going. The arc burner's blade had the water around it bubbling to a boil in seconds making it hard for him to keep his hand in place long enough to cut, but he was a stubborn bastard, and after a couple of minutes the grille fell away into the agitated broil, and we were through.

I followed Swann out, clambering up onto an aluminum deck. The room around us was vast, all concrete and steel piping, with the hissing and venting of steam providing cover for our entrance. The water was part of some sort of cooling system for the gigantic generators powering the plant. Martagan and Fate emerged from the water behind us. We took stock, dripping onto the deck. There were blast doors to the left of us, glass doors to the right. The blast doors were marked with a biohazard warning which did nothing to instill confidence in me.

The glass doors opened.

So much for the element of surprise.

I hesitated for a split second, seeing a techie step through. Swann didn't. No guns. We couldn't risk the noise being heard. His exospine meant he was capable of inhuman speed in short bursts. He was beside the man and ramming the arc burner up under his chin into his brain and catching his corpse as it slumped before I'd even finished turning toward the open door. He dragged the dead man to the side and propped him up against the wall. Swann pressed a finger against his lips and motioned for Martagan and me to go through the door and make sure the way was clear.

"Ladies first," I said. It wasn't chivalry. It was self-preservation. She was faster than me in close combat and not remotely squeamish. She broke right, I broke left, with Fate following behind us making sure no one was on our six. It was a control room, though what it was actually controlling I couldn't begin to guess. There were gauges and dials and digital readouts and an array of screens with different charts and reports scrolling across them. It was all gibberish to me. Swann moved across to the readouts, then moved down the line of the machines. He was looking for which part of the complex was drawing the most power, which the least, and all the variants in between, I realized, figuring that would take us to where we wanted to be. It was a smart way of thinking. The labs themselves would almost certainly be driving the show.

What we didn't have was a building schematic.

Coming in blind wasn't ideal. Actually, it was a long way from ideal.

"Where are we going?"

"Up," Fate said. "The lab we're after is above the cryogenics section. The place is divided into three sections, mind, body and—"

"Soul," I interrupted. He didn't laugh.

"—machine. A lot of the stuff they're working on here is A.I. related, implementing what they discover in the mind labs up on the machine floors, looking for the perfect hybrid."

"So, this chip we're after is up on the mind floors somewhere?"

"There, or if we're unlucky, it's already in the vaults." Fate said.

"This really hasn't been thought through, has it?"

"Let's just get moving, we can argue about everything later."

We backed out of the control room. As I crossed the threshold an alarm tripped, a red warning light strobing gave the air an iron-like quality. At first, I thought I'd set the alarm off somehow, but then Swann punched a couple of buttons on the keypad, and it stopped. "Our friend was late venting one of the regulators. One of the compressors overheated. Everything's fine now."

"Apart from the fact he won't be able to vent them later, either," I said.

"We'll be long gone by then," Fate assured me.

I didn't share his confidence.

Swann took the security pass from the dead techie's white coat and used it to open the blast doors. We followed him through, Fate being the last one out. Our running footsteps echoed loudly through the complex. We were confronted by a series of rising ramps that doubled back on themselves in an angular spiral, and on each platform, another set of blast doors promised access to the secrets of Akachi Corp and the Dark Continent. Some of the walls had bio scanners recessed into them, others optical ones. "We're not going to get through any of these doors without the right kind of security clearance," I said.

"I've got it covered," Fate promised, but I'd seen nothing to suggest he had.

I looked up the wide spiral of steel ramps. There was a glass ceiling dome at the top, maybe two hundred feet above my head. There were probably twenty or thirty more floors between where we were and where we almost certainly needed to be, and it didn't take a genius to realize that the security measures were going to tighten the higher we climbed.

I saw a couple of white coats walk across one of the platforms a couple of stories above.

They didn't see us, but it served as a reminder that we weren't alone in here, and we stuck out like a sore thumb. Anyone seeing us would know immediately we weren't meant to be there and would trip the alarm.

"You know what to do," Fate said to Swann. They'd obviously planned this. Swann clambered up onto the guardrail and sprung, the exospine propelling him up to the platform where the white coats were in the process of using the retina scanner to open the blast doors to the labs. He rushed up behind them, bringing the arc burner to bear, one savage thrust into the base of the spine and twist, severing the vertebrae and leaving the poor bastard gagging for a breath he couldn't take. The second white coat started to scream, but the scorching blade took out his vocal cords on the back-hand.

It never ceased to amaze me what the exospine was capable of—it transformed a cripple into one of the most prodigious killing machines I'd ever encountered.

I hadn't expected what happened next.

Swann crouched over the two men, and using the blade opened their skulls beneath the eye socket to fish the orbs out.

He waited for us to catch up.

"Now we've got clearance," Fate said, taking the eyes off his man.

I don't exactly have a sensitive stomach, but I wanted to throw up.

We continued up to the mind labs.

When he reached the blast doors, Fate held first one eye then the other up to the optical scanners and waited. The display panel went from red to green, and the doors opened.

"Party time," he said.

It was supposed to be in and out. The in, which should have been the tough part, proved to be surprisingly easy. That should have been a clue. It should have set all sorts of alarm bells ringing. The only reason it didn't was that I was so angry at Fate. Akachi had opened themselves up to us. It was as if they'd known we were coming.

Which of course they did.

That was why we didn't see more techs wandering about as we climbed up through the floors of the facility, and why we'd not triggered any of their defenses on the way in. I should have known that the whole cloaking puck trick was dumb and couldn't have worked. I'm sure they'd had eyes on us from the moment we bailed out of the Anaconda, and certainly when we were on the ground. They owned this place lock, stock, and stinky shanty. There's no way they'd just let us get this far if they hadn't got a plan to make sure we didn't walk out of there with that chip they'd no doubt invested billions in developing. I'm not stupid, sometimes I'm just a little slow.

I don't know what I'd been expecting from the lab, stacks of Petri dishes and burners maybe, but this wasn't it. The room was filled with robot arms turning and twisting as they went about the mechanized tasks of experimentation, opposable thumbs grasping the precious components as they lifted, rotated, and repositioned themselves. I couldn't see how they were being controlled, or where from, but they didn't stop what they were doing as we entered. There were a dozen stations, each of them mechanized, each assembling some separate component that would come together in a single whole.

They weren't what drew my eye. Along the wall was a dozen heavily armored men standing motionless.

Not men, I realized. They were the husks of biomechs, cyborgs if you like, androids if you're lazy. They were powered down. That didn't matter. Their presence was enough to have my heart in my throat, like it was trying to escape from inside. The biomechs were huge. They were easily seven, eight feet tall. Some sort of idealized überman. I never trusted machines. Ever. I walked across to the nearest and prodded it in the chest, hard. It didn't react.

"I thought this was supposed to be the mind lab?"

"You saw the signs," Fate said, but he sounded a little less certain.

"Signs can be changed," I said, looking around the rest of the room.

It wasn't right. This looked more like an armory than a laboratory.

Martagan didn't seem any happier than I was. She was staring at one of the robotic arms as it swiveled and pivoted and slammed two pieces of biomech tech together, fusing them. "They're building transhumans in here," she said.

I was about to contradict her and say androids when I saw the bank of glass cabinets at the far side of the room. I approached them, drawn by what was inside. Maybe this was the mind lab, but not in any way I'd expected. Inside bubbling vats of preservative were an array of brains severed from their stems, waiting to be transplanted into the artificial bodies being fashioned for them.

I rested my hand against the glass.

The others started rifling the room in search of the chip. I had no idea how it would work, some sort of interface in the base of the skull, maybe, so people could plug in, tune in and drop out.

Behind them, the robot arms carried on building, servos, valves, transistors, resistors and synthetic skin to wrap them in. Lisl Martagan was right: the machines were building a man, I realized, watching him come together in the reflection of the glass case.

It was a faster process than I could ever have imagined.

I turned away from the display case.

"It's a trap," I told Fate.

He shook his head. "No one knows we are here. Don't get your knickers in a twist."

"They were expecting us," I argued, stubbornly.

He looked up to see the final pieces slot and lock together and hear the huge electrical surge that was the machine's way of declaring let there be life. The biomech's eyes lit, and its jaw came up, jutting out aggressively. It towered over each of us. Around the room the other sentries woke one by one, lifting their right hands as if to make a vow, the joints pivoting and swiveling as the biomechs tested their fingers, running through some sort of start-up routine. We needed to move fast, before all of their systems came online.

The doors closed behind us, locking us in the lab with the biomech warriors.

"This can't be good," Martagan said, ever one for the understatement.

She wasn't wrong.

I'm all for getting stuck into a fair fight. I even enjoy an unfair one most of the time. But being locked in a small room with thirteen biomech warriors coming online at the same time didn't seem like a lot of fun. At least not for us. The biomechs were no doubt going to have the time of their lives.

Swann went for it, hurling himself across the room to hit the last one of them—the one blocking our way out—head on. The biomech didn't flinch, wobble, stagger or betray any sort of human weakness as it back-handed him away. The sound of metal on bone was sickening. His head went back. I saw the light inside his eyes go out as the incredible force of the blow lifted Swann five feet into the air and hurled him bodily into the glass display cases. The glass shattered on impact, raining bloody shards down on the fallen man. He lay there for a moment, unmoving, then slowly brought his head up, dazed, and struggled to rise. From where I was, I could see that several of the centipede legs of his exospine had been dislodged in the fall.

Swann couldn't control his legs.

It was time for us to start doing what we did best: bleed.

Martagan was the first to react.

She whipped her hand back and under-armed a knife, sending it end over end through the air to lodge in one of the biomech's optical sensors. It was a good thought; the thing had a real brain back there. The blade sank deep into metal-plated skull but didn't slow the cyborg down for a second.

It came toward us.

"What the hell have you got us into?" I yelled at Fate, but he was already engaged, fighting for his life with two of the biomechs that had closed in on him.

Thirteen seemingly indestructible warriors against the four of us.

Perfect.

Martagan ran toward one of the dangling robotic arms and launched herself up to gain height as she grabbed it. Her momentum swung it back, bringing her closer to the wall. She was running even as she hit it, her feet taking three quick steps along the wall before she pushed off and let go of the spinning arm. She hit the biomech full on.

The machine rocked back under the impact but didn't fall.

She had never intended on knocking it over.

It was all about getting close before it got its defenses online.

She slapped a magnetic proximity mine in the middle of the cyborg's chest and triggered it with a shove onto the pressure plate as it attached.

We had five seconds until it blew.

An eternity and no time at all.

We scrambled for cover as an arc of fierce blue energy rippled out from the center of the proximity mine, arcing toward the glass cabinets. The way these things work is you slam them down on the ground and the beam arcs up to the ceiling—if a droid breaks the beam, curtains. Martagan was about ten steps ahead of us, thoughtwise. I saw what she intended, and went in low for the biomech's legs, spinning it. I hit that thing with all the power of a truck, using my momentum and its weight to turn it. The arc beam sliced through the trunk of the first biomech, sheering through the cyborg's trunk and lighting its innards up like the New Year sky. The stench of burning metal and fused synth-skin was vile. It took all of my strength to keep the biomech turning, using the proximity mine's beam to slice through each of the thirteen warriors as the sizzling pulse of raw lethal energy slowly faded.

Fate hadn't moved.

He just stood there looking at the devastation, the biomech corpses twisting and twitching, trying to move, to fight on, hopelessly.

Martagan and I high-fived, slapping palms.

"Teamwork," she said.

"One gigantic clusterfuck," I said, looking at Fate.

We still hadn't found the Neurochip when the facility went into lockdown, sirens wailing, those iron-tinged lights strobing, everything so loud and bright I couldn't think.

I didn't think it could get any worse.

I was wrong.

The hit squad turned up looking for Fate.

All we could do was batten down the hatches, sit tight, defend our position.

"Tell me you have an exfiltration plan in place," I demanded.

Fate nodded. "What do you take me for? We're going to need to get up onto the roof and grab the sky hook when the Anaconda comes back around."

"How long?"

"Two hours."

"You have got to be kidding me? Two hours? We'll be dead by then."

"Better hope not," Fate said.

I hunkered down beside Swann. He didn't look good. I refrained from asking the obvious. "Anything I can do?"

"You a biomech wiz?" he asked through gritted teeth. He was sweating, pale. His legs trembled. I didn't think that was a good sign.

"I think we both know the answer to that."

"Then prop me up against the wall, give me a big fucking gun, and let me hold up the rear while you guys get out of here. They'd need more than one crew to get past me. After that, I'll take my chances."

"Not happening, bro. You can't walk. I'm not leaving you behind. Fate, tell him."

"We're all going home, or none of us are," Fate said. It was the old mantra. We all knew it off by heart. It was written on our souls.

"Very noble. Where's my gun?"

"I'm serious," I said.

"So am I," Swann countered.

It didn't matter which of us was right in the end, none of us were going anywhere.

We were surrounded on all sides. No way in or out of the lab apart from the main blast doors.

I heard something in the air ducts.

Movement.

They were either trying to sneak someone in or looking to try and smoke us out.

That, or they had a bad case of rats.

Giant oversized rats in the air ducts.

I looked around the room, taking stock of what we had. The one thing we had going for us was that the blast doors were thick. No one would be walking through them without some heavy-duty explosives to lead the way.

"We need to assume the worst, one way or another they will come through those doors eventually, so we need to dig in. Set up effective cover. Make it as difficult for them as possible. Then we need to think about how we get from here to the roof. Two hours is going to feel like a lifetime." I couldn't argue with Fate. He was on the money for once. It really was going to feel like a lifetime. "But we still haven't got what we came for. So assuming it's in here, we're finding it."

"They knew we were coming," I argued. "If this thing's that valuable, they'll have moved it to the vaults and have it under lock and key."

"Or not. Depends how arrogant the people we're up against are."

"They're company men," Swann said, grimly. "You don't get more arrogant than that."

He had a point.

I looked around again. I knew where it was. I knew where it had to be. It was the one place I wouldn't have even thought of looking a minute ago. But Swann was right, you didn't get more arrogant than some of these company men. And if you knew that, then you knew exactly where they'd hide the most precious tech in their arsenal.

It was inside the metal skull of the biomech warriors Martagan had just taken out. I was absolutely sure of it. Sure enough to stake my life on it.

"Get those barricades up," I told the others. "I know where the chip is."

I was right.

I love when I'm right.

I pulled the biomech's head away from its shoulders and started rooting around inside with my fingers, not thinking about what, exactly, it was that I was rooting around in. I felt something hard. The interface. The single part where man fused with machine.

That was where the chip was.

That was why these transhumans weren't insane. The brains inside them had been wiped of memory and personality, creating a barebones warrior capable of independent thought and action but not burdened by any of its life experiences. It was brutally efficient.

They were creating an army of modern-day zombies.

I pulled the interface out.

My fingers came out of the biomech's neck slick with mucus and blood. I turned the small black device over in my hand, looking for a way to access the chip itself, which had to be inside it.

I could just make out the metal edge of the circuitry. Using my thumbnail, I pressed it in. The spring-loader popped it out into my palm. All of this fuss over such a small thing. I shook my head.

"Got it," I said.

No one was listening to me.

The wolves were at the door.

They were at both doors, technically.

I heard the hiss of gas being pumped in through the air vents at the same time as I heard the dull metallic clang of the fragmentation bomb being affixed to the blast doors.

Things were about to get messy.

I saw curls of smoke to my right, seeping into the room from on high. I had no way of knowing if it was some sort of nerve agent that would undo us from within or something less insidious but no less lethal given the presence of the frag bomb on the door and the crew outside waiting to make mincemeat of us.

"Get Swannie," Fate said. I looked at him as he dropped something on the floor and kicked it into the center of the room. "Just do what you're told for once," he barked.

I did.

I scooped my friend up in my arms and rose.

The smoke had already formed a thick blanket above our heads and was slowly seeping down to fill the room. We were breathing it in. There was nothing we could do about that.

I heard voices beyond the blast door, muffled. No doubt screaming, "Get back!" as the detonator on the frag bomb counted down.

Fate stepped on the black plate he'd dropped, and in the silence between heartbeats and the explosive force of the blast doors being ripped apart, buckling and twisting under the intense heat of the detonation, a beam of blue light arced up, slowly beginning to solidify into a hologram-clone of Randall Fate, an M76 rocket launcher in its hands. I would have bought it, coming in through the smoke and damage. The illusion was good. But it was only going to give us a couple of seconds as the assault teams' bullets were deflected by Fate's hologram back at them. It didn't solve anything. Not really.

But Fate's one devious bastard; this was only part of the illusion.

That's why we've stuck with him for so long.

When it comes down to it, there's no one better for getting you out of a jam. He thinks about five steps ahead of the enemy. "Links hands," he yelled barely a second before the doors blew. I grabbed Martagan's outstretched had as shrapnel ripped toward us, the full force of the shockwave bowling us off our feet. We hit the floor still holding hands, but there was no smoke, no hail of debris, not smoke and fire from the blast.

We weren't in the lab.

We were back in the sub-basement where we'd come through the sewerage pipe. The rusty iron light pulsed. I felt sick. Dislocated. It took me a moment to get my bearings and grasp what Fate had done.

I knew why he'd been the last one out of the room before we'd gone up.

He'd set up a teleport.

It was a one-shot deal.

He'd known the hit squad was behind us. Only now they weren't. Now we were behind them, and they were staring at an unflinching hologram of Randall Fate and filling themselves with lead as they tried to cut it down.

Like I said, he is one devious bastard.

"We've got to get up to the roof," he said. "Marco, are you okay with Swann?" I nodded. "Okay, Lisl, you and me take point, anything moves, shoot it."

She ratcheted the pump action on her shotgun and nodded grimly.

We had the chip, we were behind enemy lines. All was good.

Apart from the fact the skyhook was still two hours away.

Teleportation, even over a couple of hundred feet always left me feeling sick.

I guess it's down to the whole matter of life being scrambled and unscrambled in the space of a heartbeat. It's disconcerting, to say the least, no matter how many times you go through it.

Fate pocketed the home plate. It wasn't like they could follow us down here when they worked out what had happened, but it was some seriously expensive kit, and the serial numbers were always traceable if you knew what you were doing and had enough money to follow the breadcrumbs through the dozens of illegal transactions that led back to our door. So he wasn't about to leave it behind and invite more trouble our way.

We didn't have long before they'd work out what we'd done, so we needed to take advantage of the few seconds he'd bought us with his bait and switch.

"We need another way up," Swann said. "Get me over to the computers, and I'll try and find us a route."

"No time," Fate disagreed. "We go up, take those bastards by surprise, and don't stop until we reach the roof."

Martagan nodded.

We hit the stairs, Fate and Martagan leading the way. I was a few steps behind them. Swann was heavy in my arms, but he was locked and loaded. He didn't need his legs working to be lethal. All I had to do was concentrate on climbing as fast as I could. He'd take care of any Bleeders who got in our way before we got to the roof.

We heard gunfire above us. They were still shooting at the fake Fate. The hologram would only last for a couple of minutes. But even the dumbest grunt would figure out what was happening long before then. There was only so much damage a man could take before he went down, whereas a hologram would stand there, unbent and defiantly unbroken even under the most intense hail of gunfire, giving every bit as good as it got for as long as the power fueling it lasted.

We rounded the next level of stairs.

Martagan fired first. No questions. No warning. No hesitation.

She put a dozen shells into the backs of the men going toe-to-toe with Fate's hologram, downing them with brutal efficiency. They didn't know what hit them. They didn't even have time to scream.

The stairwell reeked of ozone, blood, and fused metal.

I picked a careful path through the detritus of the explosion, reaching the twisted door in time to see Fate's hologram flicker and fade.

It was a mess. Huge chunks of masonry and buckled metal blocked the way, forcing us to tread carefully as we negotiated it.

The gas—whatever it was—was still pouring into the lab, choking the air.

I looked down and caught a glimpse of silver: the dog tags on the corpse closest to me had spilled out as the Bleeder fell. I dropped to one knee so Swann could snap the chain and pocket them. I wanted to know who, exactly, Fate had pissed off, because it wasn't about a crew being dispatched to take us out. No, what it *was* all about was who had dispatched them, which corporate big-wig he'd screwed with, and those dog tags were a link in the chain back to them. Follow the money, find the man who wants you dead. Just because we'd taken his team out didn't mean it was over. If anything we'd just made things ten times worse. He'd just send another wave at us and another until we were worm food.

We carried on up after the others.

Swann was heavy and getting more so every twist of the stairway. Every muscle in my back and legs burned. Breathing hard, I stopped trying to focus on anything apart from putting one foot in front of another.

He knew he was a burden, but at least he'd stopped with the nonsense about leaving him behind.

That wasn't an option.

Swann leaned over my shoulder, aiming down the sight of his G1 Jackal assault rifle back the way we'd come. If there was ever a man I wanted watching my back, it was Swann.

As we hit the roof access door, I heard cries behind us. More men were coming. Akachi's own security team, no doubt.

It wasn't over yet.

Fate used the dead white coat's eyes to circumvent security on the door. The fresh air—hot and humid—hit us like a sledgehammer. I staggered out into the bright light of the African sun.

The rooftop wasn't entirely flat; there was the glass dome in the center and various cooling vents and towers where ventilation shafts opened out onto it. Plenty of cover for our rear-guard action. We needed to set up to make sure we had all points of ingress covered. We didn't want anyone sneaking up on our six unannounced. That meant identifying the most defensible point and digging in. Martagan and Fate were already on it.

I set Swann down and propped him up with his broken back against one of the metal cooling vents with a good view of the door.

There wasn't a cloud in the sky.

There wasn't so much as a small black smudge to suggest the skyhook was on its way.

But we still had the best part of two hours left before it arrived.

"Bollocks," I muttered, erudite as ever.

I set myself up with as wide a field of vision as possible, with eyes on the door, and waited for the fun to begin.

It didn't take long for the first wave to reach us.

They were grunts. Cannon fodder. By definition, Bleeders. They weren't meant to do anything apart from keeping us busy. Six of them came spilling through the door. It was like shooting fish in a barrel. Not that I've ever shot fish in a barrel. I'm not even sure how easy it'd be to shoot fish in a barrel given the refraction and the fact they'd be swimming every which way, but you get the point. They couldn't go anywhere. Stepping through the door was suicide.

Martagan and Swann had a field day. They took turns picking the

Bleeders off, right, left, right, left. I signaled Fate. He came across to where I was hunkered down.

"This feels wrong," I said. "It's too easy."

He didn't argue with me, which is never a good sign.

"What are you thinking?"

"They're up to something. They have to be."

He nodded.

"But what?"

"If it were me, I'd blow the roof and to hell with it," I said. "They know we're digging in for evac, they also know there's no sign of the skyhook on any radar, so why waste lives needlessly? Place charges beneath us, blow the whole place to hell and us with it."

Again, he nodded. "I was thinking a little less drastic, but the same general lines." He looked over at the edge.

"You think the real force is coming up another way?"

"Almost certainly."

I crouch-ran from my cover across the rooftop to the edge and leaned over. There was a mobile platform, some sort of rig set up for keeping all of that glass sparkling, but I couldn't see anyone on it. Fate checked the other side. As he stuck his head out over the edge, it was greeted by the staccato rattle of gunfire. He pulled back, fast. Score one for Fate.

I hustled over to the other side to join him.

They were climbing up the glass, friction gloves meaning they could move fast, like spiders, but the gloves needed to be in contact with the glass to stop them from falling. Metaphorically, at least, they had to fight with one hand behind their backs. I'd take any advantage on offer. I'm not proud. I'm also practical. They'd fragged us in there. I felt it was only fair to return the compliment. I unclipped one of the three grenades from my belt and pulled the pin. There was a ten-second timer on it. I released the trigger, counting to eight, then dropped it over the side. It bounced off the glass. A second later it blew, taking the side of the building and the Bleeders coming up the glass wall with it. I felt the heat of the explosion on my skin and turned in time to see Swann put down the last of the first wave with a single bullet to the throat. He was showing off. The man didn't die immediately. He squirmed on the rooftop, clutching at his neck trying to stop the air from leaking out of the gaping hole Swann's bullet had made and then trying to block it long enough to suck down another breath as he struggled to inhale.

The sound of wet flesh slopping about between his fingers was music to my ears.

I stood on his skull, putting him out of his misery, and piled the six corpses up to make a barricade.

In the few minutes respite, we took stock of the situation.

We weren't helpless. We'd got some serious kit with us, including my favorite toy. It cost a small fortune, we're talking serious black-market tech that involved crossing more than a few greasy palms with silver, but in practice, it's worth every single dime spent on it. It's built into the weave of my suit. All I have to do is trigger it, and it emits an electromagnetic pulse that screws with targeting and threat sensors—that's the joy of intelligent weapons, they can be pretty damn stupid at times—and winds up having Bleeders shooting at their own crew. What's not to love?

"Bring 'em on," I said, patting my chest.

Fate knew what I had in mind.

He approved.

I stood behind the barricade of corpses waiting for the second wave, ready to raise some hell.

I could hear them on the stairs.

I knew they wouldn't just come pouring out through the door this time.

Things were about to get interesting.

Something came rolling out through the doorway. For one sickening second, I thought it was a frag bomb. It wasn't.

It might have been better if it had been.

I launched a blistering barrage of shots that should have cut them in half.

Thirty men streamed out through the door, and my bullets weren't doing anything. Beside me, Swann and Martagan were having no more joy.

I saw the line of used shells filling up on the rooftop, and it really was a line, like the shots had hit a wall and simply fallen in defiance of any kind of physics I understood.

I knew what had come rolling out through the doorway: a deployable force field. It wouldn't last forever, but right now it was giving them the perfect cover to storm the rooftop.

I turned momentarily to scan the horizon looking for any sign of rescue. I'd have had more luck if I was out hunting a unicorn. No doubt about it. We were in the shit way up over our heads.

"I have absolutely no intention of dying here," I said. It was becoming a mantra. I don't think the universe believed me.

This time Fate had no witty one-liner comeback, a sure sign things were grim.

There was no way we could hold the roof for the best part of two hours. I'm a born optimist, but even I'm not blind. The second that shield fell we were finished.

Thinking fast I pulled the second frag bomb from the clip and pulled the pin. I saw the look of abject terror on Randall Fate's face, and I don't mind admitting I enjoyed it just a little bit. He thought I was going to hurl it at the invisible barrier and blow us all to kingdom come. I'm not an idiot. I had something else in mind entirely. Unfortunately, we didn't have ropes or belay pins which would have made it a lot easier. No. That wasn't true, we did have ropes. Thick cables were dangling off the side of the building where I'd already blown the window cleaner's platform to hell. It was all coming together. I didn't throw the frag grenade, I ran around to the far side of the glass dome and set it down, releasing the handle in the process. I had ten seconds to get as far away as possible, which meant the other side of the glass dome, knowing it was about to unleash a molten hell of razor-sharp glass shards and shred anything unlucky enough to get in their way. Clowns with guns to the left, death by fire and glass to the right. Some choice.

"Down!" I yelled.

They didn't need telling twice.

The explosion ripped through the glass dome, what remained crumpling inwards. Most of the glass fell rather than flew, so it rained down on the atrium far below instead of cutting into us and left a huge sinkhole that plunged all the way down to the sub-basement hundreds of meters down. Suddenly we had choices. "Help me with the ropes," I yelled at Fate, my ears ringing. I couldn't hear any answer. He was on his feet and following me, dusting off the debris that had showered him. Sometimes, with a good crew, the link is almost telepathic. You just know what the other person needs. Martagan and Swann made damned sure no one was sneaking around the edge of the force wall while Fate and I hauled up the steel ropes that dangled from the heavy winch and threw them down the sinkhole in the center of the building.

I sent Fate over the side.

I looked at Swann. "Can you do it?"

"One way to find out," he said, bleakly. He was right, of course. I couldn't carry him down and climb. The exospine gave him incredible upper body strength, assuming none of the centipede interfaces that locked into the upper vertebrae had been dislodged or broken in the biomech warrior's attack. If they had evolution had about a nanosecond to fashion wings for him before he hit terminal velocity. He slung the assault rifle over his shoulder, and I carried him to the edge. Shots rang out behind me. Martagan laying down covering fire. I sat Swann down on the edge. He grasped the thick steel rope and slid out over the side. I turned my back. I couldn't look. Two men were trying to work their way around the extremes of the force field, but Lisl had them covered. She was like me. She enjoyed it when things got rough.

I expected Swann to scream, but after a couple of seconds without the tell-tale muffled crump of impact, I focussed on what still needed to be done up here.

I laid down covering fire for Martagan as she retreated to the shattered dome.

"Ladies first," she said.

Who was I to argue?

The steel rope twisted around in my hands like a live snake.

The weight of the others and their frantic downward scramble made it almost impossible to hang on as it bucked and thrashed. In a perfect world, we'd have had those easy catch-and-release clamps and basically rappelled down the shaft in a couple of seconds, no damage to our hands in the process. No such luck. And it was a long way down.

Losing my grip wasn't an option.

The thick coil of rope didn't stretch all the way down to the ground. There was a winch up top that was used to raise and lower the window cleaner's platform. It was mechanized, but I was banking on it spooling out more steel rope as we descended, our weight too much for the lock. There's a delicate balance when it comes to desperate measures. Too much give in the mechanism would have us hurtling to the ground.

As it was, we weren't going down fast enough.

Gritting my teeth, I pushed on, one eye on the edge of the dome, expecting to see the enemy crews leaning out over it at any second.

We were a long way from the balustrades on every story. There was no way to just reach out and grab one without turning the steel rope into a giant pendulum.

My shoulders burned from the hand-over-hand descent. The abrasive steel fibers scored my palms, filaments cutting deep into the skin. I wrapped my ankles around the rope and tried to slide a few feet at a time, but going down the rope that way tore mercilessly away at my palms. I kept on going down, urging the others to go faster. Whatever damage was done could always be fixed. Being dead couldn't. I'm not some sort of pro-human lobbyist. I don't believe natural is best. I've got absolutely no problem with synth skin on my palms, or manskin as I think they call it these days, even if I burned the flesh down to the bone. Better that than the alternative. Always.

Two stories.

Four.

Six.

Eight.

Ten.

Every new hold from the guys below me had the rope bucking against my grip, the motion exaggerated by the pull of gravity. Clinging on grew more and more difficult for every story we descended, the blood from my hands making it virtually impossible to grip. And then the winch gave way, the lock breaking, and the rope unraveled faster than we could climb.

The ground rushed up toward us. And we plunged down toward it.

Fifteen.

Twenty.

Thirty.

I screamed as I went down, the steel burning through my grip. The agony was incredible, turning the world to black. It was all I could do to cling on to the rope—right up until the moment it ran out, and there was no more length to give. As we hit the end of it, the entire rig hit a dead stop, the jarring impact almost as bad as if we'd hit the concrete still five floors below.

My hands were shredded, slick with blood. I didn't dare to look, knowing I'd see bone. I didn't even want to think about what had to happen next; assuming we got off the rope, I was going to have to carry Swann out of there with my ruined hands. The pain was excruciating.

I slithered down another few feet, trying to lock myself off with my ankles before I fell.

The shaft reeked of burned flesh.

Ours.

Below me, Fate kicked out, setting the pendulum into motion. It took five arcs before the rope was moving enough for him to reach out to the lowest balcony, and even as he caught it, our combined weight was working to pull him away from safety. But Fate was stubborn. He didn't like losing any more than I did. He anchored us in place, allowing us to climb over him to safety.

Well, dubious safety. We were still five floors up, a long way from where the skyhook was meant to pick us up, and a long way from the pipeline we'd crept into Akachi through. We were in no man's land. But at least we'd survived a few more minutes. That was something.

Sometimes a gig gets complicated by circumstances outside of your control.

Sometimes you just have to make it more complicated because an opportunity arises.

Sometimes those opportunities seem to be too good to be true for a reason.

Like this one.

We opened a door.

On the other side of it, we found a man who, given the genius of his biomech personality rewriting chip technology, might as well have been God. Mankind spent centuries creating an all seeing all powerful deity capable of magic, of creation, and then spent just as long stripping the invisible one of His powers, but the one thing it had never been able to do outside of a Petri dish was create life. Until now. Aldus Keyes was his name. It wasn't just about storing information that could be accessed, or developing skill sets the man with the chip interfaced with his brainstem had hitherto been incapable of, or even boosting intelligence with processing power, fusing man and machine in some biomech transhuman. It was all about fashioning a brand new personality. A new man. Giving flesh a soul, if you like, which was, of course, the last bastion of the god they'd created for themselves. We didn't know that at the time, of course. He was just a white coat. A shield we could hide behind when the bullets started flying.

Fate gambled that he was our ticket out of the place; that they wouldn't risk killing him.

Unlike Fate, I wasn't sure they'd risk losing him, either.

He was a small man, with little in the way of defining marks or memorable features; indeed he seemed almost to have rewritten his flesh into absolute and unremarkable averageness in the same way that his discovery was capable of rewriting the insides of the mind.

He didn't put up a fight.

Recalling what had happened to the two other white coats on the landing earlier, that was perhaps for the best.

Martagan cuffed him and escorted him to the stairs.

Fate blocked out our escape route, running point.

I struggled with Swann. I wouldn't leave him, despite his protestations, but the mess of my hands made carrying him torture. I looked up as we stepped out into the atrium beneath the shattered dome, broken glass crunching beneath my feet. Black-clothed operatives streamed down the levels, the glo-lights on their suits eerie in the shadows. I didn't need to count them. We were outnumbered. Badly.

But this was far from over.

What they didn't know as they streamed down toward us was that the odds had just tilted dramatically in our favor. Fate grabbed the unassuming scientist by the throat and crushed his windpipe, making it hard for him to answer the question he posed, "How do we get out of here?" Keyes hacked and hocked, trying to get a breath and somehow squeeze the words Fate wanted to hear out past his opposable thumbs. Fate relented just long enough for him to gasp two words, "That way," and point.

"This way?" Fate demanded.

The man nodded desperately. He really was a wretched creature.

"Then this way it is. You first." He pushed the scientist a couple of steps ahead, using him as a human shield, as we made our way toward the ground floor and an enormous foyer with ice sculptures that existed purely because they could, to serve as a way of Akachi reinforcing just how rich they were compared with their poor neighbors. The sculptures were representations of animals that had long since ceased to roam the Serengeti. They took up positions beneath, behind and between them, the huge glass doors behind them locked down. They were inches from freedom. But those doors weren't moving for love nor money.

Things were about to get really crowded down there.

"Tell them we're walking out of here, Mister Scientist Man," Fate said. "Nice and easy. We don't want any itchy trigger fingers."

"Stay back," the man shouted, his call filling the foyer. There was nothing timid about his voice now. They listened to him. Fate saw that, realized exactly what it meant and was already processing the next stages of our exfiltration.

"We can't do that, sir," one of the security force called back.

"Yes, you can. I'm telling you to do that, and you're going to do what I tell you."

"No can do, Professor Keyes. Our orders are that these men don't leave the facility alive."

"And I'm giving you new orders, soldier. Open the doors. This doesn't have to turn into a blood bath. You know who I am. You know what I'm worth. It's all about money. It always is with these people. You have their faces, their bioscans, everything there is to know about them is at your fingertips. Use it to bring me home. I'll walk out here with these men. Your job is to find me. Understood?"

"Negative, Professor. We can't let that happen."

"You have no choice," Fate barked, his voice filling the cavernous space. He turned to the scientist. "How do we get through the doors?"

"I don't know," the white coat said. "Not now the building's on lockdown. It's a smart building. It's protecting itself."

I believed him. Luckily for all concerned, I knew exactly how we'd get through them. "I do," I said, tapping the one remaining frag bomb on my belt. Can't open a door? Make a new one. Why complicate life?

What I hadn't considered was the damage done to the tower's frame by the two previous fragmentation bombs I'd detonated in the last couple of minutes, one of which had taken a huge bite out of the side of the tower and changed its structural integrity. The engineering and mathematics behind these super towers is nothing short of wizardry. The thing is, screw with one side of the equation, the ramifications will just be exacerbated on the other. Meaning, quite literally, that by taking a chunk out of the side of the tower from around the twentieth to thirty-third floors, I'd undermined the basic physics that kept the building upright.

Another well-placed charge and the whole thing was coming down around our ears. One thing I'm getting very good at is blowing shit up. It's a gift.

The problem was I couldn't just place the charge against the glass and back away. There was nowhere for us to take cover. Letting a frag bomb off in close proximity was like buying a lottery ticket where there was a prize every time. Most of them, of course, involved various gruesome deformities and reduced life expectancy.

I thought very seriously about taking out a couple of the snipers the security detail had lined up, figuring that I could lay their corpses over the frag bomb and dampen the effect of it a little. The truth was it wouldn't do much apart from spray out bloody 'rain' across the foyer.

There were, however, ice sculptures.

But that would mean risking turning our backs to the trigger happy security detail.

And, to be honest, something the Professor had said had got me spooked: we were in a smart building, on lockdown... and it was protecting itself? I really didn't like the sound of that.

In the end, it wasn't my decision to make.

I saw guide ropes hit the ground and realized another crew was rappelling down the front of the building to cut us off from escape. That hustled me along. With Swann still clinging to my back—I couldn't hold him because of the damage done to my hands—I crab-ran to the nearest sculpture, a towering fish salmon-leaping out of a spray of water, something much bigger rising up behind it to feast, and using all my strength, put my weight behind it and pushed it across the marble floor to where I intended to lay the frag bomb. I repeated it with two more—a phoenix rising from crystal blue flames, and what appeared to be a slowly melting unicorn, up on its rear legs, kicking the air. The three between them ought to be enough to shield us from the blast.

Fate didn't move. He had the barrel of his gun pressed hard into the Professor's temple, using the white coat a human shield, his free arm wrapped around the smaller man's shoulders, pinning him.

Beside him, Lisl Martagan had all angles covered.

The first men came into view, bouncing down the glass superstructure, as I set the final frag bomb in place and backed away.

The next ten seconds were the longest of my life.

I knew, right around the fifth, that there was no way the ice would absorb enough of the blast, and would instead hurl lethal dagger-sharp slivers at us, perforating our bodies like a pin cushion. With three seconds left, I knew I had to run, but with Swann clinging on to my neck, a literal monkey on my back, I knew I wasn't going anywhere.

With two seconds left I saw the red dot on my chest.

And with one second left, I threw myself to the deck, beating the bullet and the blast by milliseconds.

Instinctively, I put my hands out to break my fall.

Mistake.

Big fucking mistake.

I screamed, but the air and sound were sucked out of my lungs by the detonation.

I felt ice rip across my legs—not my back, Swann had that covered. I heard the whimpers of pain in my ear as the shards bit through his exospine. But he was breathing, and I was breathing and in my book that was a win. We had a gaping hole to walk out through. Who needed more?

We walked out of that place, Fate shoving Professor Keyes ahead of us, which in Fate's world made the mission a success. I'm a little more glass is half empty when it comes to getting shot at, blown up, charring the skin off my palms and otherwise having a bad day, myself.

My brain was rocking to the tune of tinnitus.

Something didn't feel right.

It was in the foundations, rippling like an earthquake. The ground couldn't be trusted.

"Move!" I yelled, no idea how loudly because I couldn't hear anything.

I didn't need to.

I could feel it.

My frag bomb had blown out the load-bearing glass wall, and combined with the damage done up top and internally, the metal skeleton couldn't hold and was twisting out of true. That's a fancy way of saying the entire thing was coming down.

So much for a quick in-and-out.

The money men at Akachi Corp had just moved our gang of four right to the top of their Most Wanted list.

We staggered out into the oasis and kept on going, eyes on the sky.

The skyhook was coming.

PART TWO

THE DEATH OF FATE

Fate found me in a Beetle den in Old Tokyo.

I wasn't in a good way. The op to re-skin my hands had been a success, but the meds were like old friends. Friends who really didn't know when to take the hint and just fuck off. It wasn't a seedy place. The girls, modern equivalents of geishas, I guess, moved in and out of the private rooms, all beauty and grace, bringing the delicious hit with them. Some patrons would go for twofers, combining guilty pleasures. Everything was for sale, after all. Me, I just curled up on the red velvet couch and stared at the walls, scratching my arms and sweating—and swearing too. Lots of that. Inventive stuff and fused body parts and rodents, that kind of thing. That was the climb down. I hated that. You'd think after all these years the scientists would have done something useful like crack the mystery of a controlled high, non-addictive, non-degenerative, non-anything exciting basically. But even if they did, people would still crawl to dens like Missy Tohe's.

He came banging on the door, all apologies and promises.

I didn't want to listen.

"One last job, Marco. You owe us. We're a team. We can't do it without you."

"Haven't I heard that before?" I said, scratching. My skin was crawling, and not just from the drug. Being around Fate did that to me now.

"This is different."

"It was last time, too."

"You owe us, Marco. I don't care if you've found religion or just want to lose yourself in this shit for the rest of your life, right now, today, you owe us. You're part of this. An emissary from Akachi turned up at our door—"

"You killed him, I take it?"

Fate shook his head. "It wasn't like that. They don't want to hurt us. They want to hire us. We're the guys who brought down an entire secret high-security facility in Africa, dude. We're fucking legends at their place. We're the guys who didn't just steal their fancy Neurochip, we stole the scientist who created the damned thing. And now they want to hire us to bring him back! You've got to love it, right? We broke their system, they want us to fix it. Delicious irony."

"Or they just want to make sure we're killed this time," I said, ever the optimist.

"Seriously, man, you could buy yourself a small island, the kind of money they're offering. Swann won't go in without you. Reckons you're his good luck charm."

"Or his donkey," I said, but I smiled this time when I said it, which Fate interpreted as a sign of weakness.

"Yeah, well, Martagan's less enthused, but she thinks the same way I do, we're a team. All for one, one for all. We started this together, we end it the same way. Or we don't do it at all."

"Then I vote for not doing it at all."

Before he could answer a sunken-eyed girl came in with a silver tray to offer Fate a hit. He declined with a pleasant enough smile, but she insisted, "You want to be here, you pay to be here," so he gave her a few bucks for a hit and passed the stuff over to me. "Call it an early Christmas present."

I took it off him. I'm not proud.

She left us alone again.

"You don't see what's wrong with this?" I asked the moment the door closed behind her. "We're biting the hand that feeds. That's never smart. You're talking about going into GenX, stealing the Professor right out from under their noses. You don't need to be a Flatliner to know that's not going to end well." Flatliners were a new breed of tech warrior, willing to stop their own hearts to enter that in-between place. By dying they basically become part of the machine, ghosts in there, capable of all sorts of very scary shit. They only have a couple of minutes to do whatever hack they've been sent in to do, but in those two minutes they're capable of pretty much anything, or so I've heard. I don't claim to understand it really. Guns and violence I understand. Wanting to literally become part of some giant hive-mind machine? Not so much.

"That's the beauty of it, we set up a meet with our guy at GenX, and then we just walk in the front door, no need for anything fancy. No cunning plans to circumvent security. They'll greet us with open arms. If we do it right, we won't even need to fire a single shot. They won't expect us to turn on them."

"But why us? Why should we get involved?"

"Like I said, we're the team that took Akachi down, they want to hire the best, that's us." So they'd pandered to his vanity. Made sense. It's exactly what I would have done. I unwrapped the little sachet of Beetle and rubbed the gel into the thin skin on the inside of my elbow where the veins were closest to the surface. No need for needles or any other junkie paraphernalia. "According to their guy, it's personal for them. It isn't just about losing the tech, which was a major body blow, obviously. It's about what GenX intend to use it for, that's what's really got their panties in a bunch."

"I'm going to regret asking, aren't I? But what do GenX intend to use this miraculous discovery for? Not to end world hunger I assume?"

"Stage one is destroying the existing power structures around the world, taking down rival corps, and replacing them with GenX controlled systems. It's insidious. All pervasive. Think about it. Every platform linked back in some way to GenX. Every terminal. Every machine. They'd control the world. It's bad enough as it is now, a few rival corps basically telling when we eat, when we drink, when we shit and when we sleep, but if it's only one, it's so much worse because it opens the way to stage two." I listened to his paranoid bullshit. I'd heard it all before, or variants of it, at least. Fate gobbled up this conspiracy theory stuff. "And that's when they start brainwashing and re-programming everyone, from the lowest echelons of society on up. That's why they wanted to get their hands on the Akachi chip that Aldus Keyes invented. It's not about reprogramming criminals so they can reintegrate into society and become useful. It's all about control, and where better to start than in their base of operations, where the buildings themselves have been uprooted and cleansed and stripped of all disease and decay? Yep, that's the plan, they're going to turn every single one of their employees into a genuine motherfucking corporate drone. Are you really going to sit around and let that happen? Don't try and tell me you are, Marco. I know you. You're a fucking idealist. This is the kind of shit that makes your blood boil. Embrace your anti-establishment soul, my friend."

"You do realize what this sounds like, right? Whacko conspiracy theory shit, which of course I know is your favorite kind, but still... it's a stretch."

"You were in that lab with us. You plucked the chip out of that biomech's brain. You know this stuff works. That's not conspiracy, my friend, that's cold hard fact. And I don't mind telling you, I don't want to live in a world where one corp holds all the aces. People like me and you, we'll be the first ones wiped. Our DNA's all over GenX databases. They'll turn us into nice little drone soldiers. Is that what you want?"

I thought about it. The Beetle didn't help me focus. I was jumpy and irritated and really just wanted to close my eyes and enjoy the high before the climb down, and the inevitable withdrawal shakes, pounding head, creeping flesh and all the not-so-fun stuff that went with the habit. The thing is, he was right. I don't like the corporate system. I don't like the way money makes our world go round. I don't like the way we've ceded control of our lives over to these massive corporations and put our trust in them when all they care about is the bottom line. I feel like some kind of anarchist railing against the system, but the truth is our little crews, our four-man teams, feel like they should be a microcosm of what society ought to be, a team where we all look out for each other. That shouldn't be so difficult, should it?

"If I do this, we're done, Fate. All debts paid off in full. We're quits. I can't keep doing this. We've gone beyond being smart. Now we're just riding our luck, and that's going to run out. We both know it. Going toe-to-toe with GenX? That's suicidal. But you're right, we're a team. So, we're talking one last hurrah. That's the only way this is going down. I want that island in the sun, sure, but more importantly, I want to be alive to enjoy it."

"Sure. Absolutely. I'm with you, man. Growing old's where it's at."

"I said *if*. That doesn't mean I will."

But of course it did. For old debts, for old friendships, for a clean slate. I understand exactly what the true nature of a crew is. I always have. Family. You can't always choose your family, but you stick with them when the shit hits the fan. A gig needs all of the unique gifts we bring to the table. Getting out of the GenX Inc. labs was going to be no different.

Fate was right for once.

We just walked right on in through the front door.

It was three days after Fate had come looking for me. I hadn't exactly been in a hurry to leave Missy Tohe's. I'd even broken one of my rules and taken advantage of more of the delights the Beetle den had on offer, including the lovely Amina, one of Missy's girls, who was only too happy to try and blow the blues away. She didn't exactly rock my world, but given I expected to die within a few minutes of walking into GenX, I figured it was better to go out empty rather than fully loaded, so to speak.

We were supposed to meet with a new guy, Auster, who was handling contracts on the Former United States of America side of things. We'd never met him before. Which of course accounted for the fact that none of us had a clue that he was a she. A particularly well-dressed powerbroker of a she, in point of fact, who didn't look all that pleased to see us. But then we had just walked into her office in full combat gear, carrying far too much equipment for a social call. She might spend most of her life surrounded by paperclips and hole punches, but even a pen pusher like Miss Auster could tell this wasn't the social call Fate had pretended it was.

She closed the door behind her and invited us to take a seat at the big table.

The office was chrome and glass, sterile and angular. There were thirty seats around a huge conference table and no art on the walls. There was a giant screen at the head of the room, which was black, and speakers on the table that were no doubt for relaying the whims of whatever face filled that screen when it mattered. We, quite obviously, didn't matter, and Auster made no bones about it.

"I'll admit I'm a little unsure why you were so intent on meeting like this," she said, not sitting. She leaned on the mahogany table, putting her weight on her knuckles as she leaned forward, offering a tantalizing glimpse of cleavage. I'll admit it improved my mood. "Obviously everyone here is appreciative of the work you've done for us in the past, but after events out in Africa, it's perhaps best if you keep a low profile for a while, no? You're hot, and not in a good way."

That was hard to argue with, but Fate decided it was his job to do just that. "On the contrary, right now is when you should be standing beside us, offering us more work, making a show of just how much you value us. We just walked into Akachi territory and walked out again with one of their prize boffins. Who else could have done that?"

"Several teams that we've got on the books currently," she said, bluntly. "And most of them would have made a lot less mess in the process."

"Easy to say, but with all due respect, you weren't there. We did what we had to do, and I don't mind saying we did a pretty a good job of it, all things considered."

"And you were well compensated for it. What do you want, a pat on the back?"

I laughed at that. I was beginning to like this Auster woman. She had Fate's number. Fate glared at me. Lisl Martagan smirked. Swann hadn't taken his eyes of Auster since she met us at the door. It wasn't exactly love-at-first-sight, but he was definitely smitten.

"No, it's all right. What I want is a job. A high profile job. Something worthy of what we've done for GenX so far. Something that says we're your go-to guys."

It was a risky gambit, all she had to say was no, we don't need you, and we were out of there, and we still didn't have any idea where they were keeping Aldus Keyes.

"I don't think that's a good idea," she said.

"There are others out there who want our services, you do understand that, right? We're hot property right now in the best way. There are plenty of corps who'd pay big money to have us on their side. After all, we know where the bodies are buried, if you catch my drift?"

"Is that a threat, Mister Fate?"

"More of an observation."

"I can't say I particularly appreciate your 'observation,'" she said.

"But I shall take it under advisement. But the fact remains, there's nothing for you to do."

"I beg to differ," Fate said. She raised an eyebrow. I've never seen someone actually do that. "I happen to know that Akachi are looking to even things up with you. They've put a rather large contract out on GenX, specifically to get back their man, but also to put an end to the threat they believe you pose," that wasn't part of the script. Fate had gone off message. I really didn't like the way this was going.

"Is that so?" He had her interest.

He had mine too.

I don't know what he hoped to accomplish, but he'd pretty much just told her we'd been offered obscene amounts of money to turn on her people, and what, precisely it was that Akachi hoped to achieve by hiring us.

I stared at him.

He wasn't blinking.

"You have my word."

"And how, may I ask, can you be sure of this?" She was fishing.

He bit. "Because we were the first people they came to."

"Let me get this straight, you've been hired to steal back Professor Keyes and his Neurochip? Am I understanding this correctly?"

Fate nodded.

"And you've got the brass balls to come in here and tell me to my face?" She sounded like she genuinely admired his idiocy.

I'm not afraid of death—it's hard to be and do the job I do. But I have to admit, I'm not actually looking forward to the dying part.

And that, right then, felt a whole lot closer than it had even an hour ago.

I should have stayed in that Beetle den in Old Tokyo. Sometimes you don't need to come home. Especially when this is the kind of shit you're coming home to.

"You have to admire that in a man," Fate said.

She didn't seem to agree.

"What's to stop me just calling security in and having you ended right here, right now?"

"Well, I'll be honest, I was hoping you'd make a counteroffer," Fate said.

"Were you now? Well, I might just have something of interest, but that rather depends on you, and just how willing you are to commit to our cause."

The offer wasn't what any of us expected.

Or wanted.

When she said how willing, what she was really saying was: *are you ours, body and soul?*

We were given the royal treatment. Auster had an escort of ten men come to walk us down. That should have been a clue. Fate seemed oblivious to the implications of it, happily chatting to the woman as she led the way. GenX was the antithesis of Akachi's facility. It was all sterile and white, like a new age hospital, white doors flush to white walls so that you wouldn't have seen them if you didn't know they were there. There were shuttles and glass elevators and a swarm of people moving through the place muttering. I overheard snatches of conversation that made precious little sense. One such involved bees and how the boffin thought he'd cracked a pseudo-pollination technique that would remove our dependence upon the humble bumble bee with a manmade corn-wheat crossbred. He seemed very excited. His partner not so much. But of course, a world without bees was something we were all having to come to terms with. It's part of the whole evolution of the species and survival of the fittest. We needed to adapt, and that's exactly what these white coats were trying to do, adapt. Of course, it was all GMOs now—genetically modified food. You can't taste the difference no matter how many hormones have been pumped into your prime rib to make it big and juicy, and given the insane population spiral of the last fifty years, there's simply no way a non-GMO world would do anything but starve.

I followed them down, my head full of razor blade thoughts that cut into me repeatedly.

Auster and her team led us to a secure area, Level 10, inside the facility. She needed to prove her identity at the door with a full body biometric scan. The intimation was that whatever went on behind that door was seriously classified, Eyes Only stuff. I wasn't sure that seeing it was going to help our case.

The door opened.

Fate followed Auster inside.

I looked at Swann. He just shrugged. The operation to repair his exospine had been rough, apparently. There'd been some serious damage to the vertebrae interfaces that the centipede legs anchored into, but the docs had the power to rebuild him, and Swann had the money to pay for a few enhancements to the rig along the way. He joked that he was Swann 2.0.

We went in side-by-side.

I don't know what I'd expected, but we walked into a huge vault of stasis chambers, thousands upon thousands of them lined up, stretching as far as the eye could see. Behind the glass, in each one, I saw a face. Blank. Unknowing. Men, women, big, small, grotesquely obese, anorexically thin and all the shapes and sizes in between.

"Our guinea pigs," Auster said, proudly. "The dregs of society. Everyone in here has been judged and found guilty of some vile crime against humanity," what she really meant, I was sure, was the corporation, but that was splitting hairs. "In here we aim to rehabilitate them so that they can become once again valuable members of society."

"You mean you're wiping their personalities," Martagan said, less than impressed.

"It's more complicated than that, my dear, but if we're speaking crudely, then yes."

There were hundreds of them in here. Thousands.

"How does it work?" Fate asked. It wasn't the question that would have been top of my priorities—that would have been why have you brought us in here? Because I already had a good idea what Auster had meant when she asked how willing we were to commit to their cause.

"It's painless. They know nothing about it, believe me. We're not animals."

"No," I said softly, "but you treat them as if they are."

"Let's cut to the chase, shall we? Obviously, this is meant to intimidate us," Martagan said. "So let me just state for the record I'm not intimidated in the slightest. I'm not even particularly curious. So make your counter offer and then we can go about doing what we've been hired to do. After all, it's only business, right? Nothing personal."

"Quite," Auster said. "I have been authorized to make the following offer. I advise you to think it over carefully before you answer. It's a one-time offer. We would like you to join us, to lead our team of Sleepers."

I looked at the blank faces in the glass cases. The one thing they weren't doing is sleeping.

"We have developed a revolutionary command structure," Auster continued. You will become four of the most powerful people in the world, with an army at your disposal."

"An unthinking, unquestioning army," Martagan said, cutting to the chase. "So why do you need us? Why not just wind them up and point them in the right direction for whatever war it is you want to start?"

"The Sleepers are linked—even now they are in constant communication with each other, networked on a cerebral level. We have you to thank for this development. Did you know that? Yes, it's amazing what you can do when someone brings you the missing link. Suddenly the gap between hope and understanding is bridged, and your dream of a drone army becomes a reality. So thank you. Without Professor Keyes' marvelous invention we never would be in a position to do this. Now we have the means to control the neural highways and byways in a virtual network, all linking back to a single controlling mind." I really didn't like the way this was going. I knew what the offer was going to be before she spelled it out. It was an offer you couldn't refuse but absolutely had to. "We want you to be that controlling mind."

And there it was.

The rock and the hard place crushing in around us.

The devil and the deep blue sea looking to drown us in a fiery ocean of shit.

Or more basically, we had a choice: to be the fucked or the absolutely fucking fucked. It wasn't much of a choice.

"And if we say no?"

"Then we must, unfortunately, terminate our arrangement."

The inference was 'with extreme prejudice, meaning a bullet to the head, which is how all the best people terminate arrangements.

"I'm going to have to say no," Fate said, moving faster than I've seen him move in years. He was behind Auster and had her in a headlock, the muzzle of his Vent HK01 pressed up against her temple before she could give the signal for her goons to attack.

Or so he thought.

There was a soft click that was amplified as it was repeated not once, not one hundred times, but thousands of times throughout the vault, the click followed by a steam-hiss of pressurized air venting out of the glass coffins.

We were in trouble.

Big trouble.

"That is a pity," she said. "I had such high hopes for you." She didn't move to free herself and showed no sign of discomfort or panic. "Kill them all," she said, vocalizing the order for our benefit, I'm sure.

It was effective. The glass coffins opened and slowly the Sleepers began to emerge from their hibernation.

"I'm thinking this wasn't the best plan you've ever had," Swann said, beside me. Gallows humor. You tend to do that as a Bleeder. Making jokes about the inevitability of death is the only thing that keeps you sane after a while.

"Oh, I don't know," I said, "I think this is one of his better ideas myself."

The synchronized marching feet was unerring, bare feet slapping on the marble floor. It took me a second to realize these drone soldiers weren't armed. Not that they needed an arsenal to take us out. There were thousands of them and four of us. They could tear us limb from limb, and there was nothing we could do about it. No matter how many we took out a dozen more would rise to take the place of the fallen. They'd swarm over us.

It wasn't the way I'd imagined going out.

That had always been a blaze of glory kind of deal, plenty of last-ditch heroics and snappy one-liners that made it look like I was laughing in the face of death, not shitting myself at the prospect of being drawn and quartered by a zombie horde.

How did you take out several thousand mindless warriors all at once?

I wish I knew.

Fate had his own ideas.

He pulled the trigger.

The side of Auster's head opened up, spraying blood, bone, and gristle across the nearest Sleeper as her body buckled in his arms.

I couldn't believe it.

But it made sense: if she was controlling the army with her mind the only way to call them off was to sever the connection. Killing her was the fastest way to do that.

Some of the slop from her brain landed at my feet with a wet squelch.

I looked down at it, then up at the nearest Sleeper, hoping to hell the lights had gone out in its head.

It stared back at me blindly.

I looked at Fate.

He was grinning like an idiot.

He seemed to have completely forgotten that a dozen of the men who'd accompanied us down here to Level 10's glass coffins weren't tied to the hive mind.

This wasn't what we'd planned. Not even remotely. We'd just made some very bad enemies. We'd fucked up any chance we had of coming good as far as Akachi's objectives went, and we'd painted a big target on our backs as far as GenX were concerned. We were running out of allies. We'd got Ayako-Mizuki out in Asia, who were all about reaching for the sun if you swallowed the corporate line. Their focus was off-world exploration. Not sure where we could fit in there. Then there was Warwulf-Blaze, commodity traders who basically ruled Fortress Europe. Avalon, a security corporation set up in a no longer Great Britain, which was probably our last real shot at a lasting friendship, but that meant rain and lots of it, steel grey skies and constant depression, but that was better than the afterlife, or Kuznetzov, energy solutions operating out of the autocratic Russian Steppes and then we were shit out of luck, and out of friendly corps. We were making enemies far too quickly.

"I hope you've got a plan for how we get out of here," I said as Fate's eyes opened wide—impossibly wide—and his jaw dropped open. I looked down and saw the arc-blade protruding from Auster's stomach. One of Auster's goons had rammed it through him and her, opening them wide. He lost his grip on her. She slumped, sliding off the end of the blade. Fate sank to his knees.

I stared at him as he fell forward, landing on top of the woman.

Then there were three.

Three people trapped in the middle of hostile territory, two corpses at their feet, ten very angry men around them intent on fulfilling their mistress's last order. Ten men. Three of us. Forget all of the Sleepers surrounding. It all came down to ten men. And against ten men I'd back us any time.

I reached down, drawing twin blades from the sheaths in my boots, and threw them hard, end-over-end into the throat and stomach of the two men closest to me. Brutal. Efficient. No hanging around waiting for them to act first. We needed to get out of there. Now it was three against eight. And it was about to get a lot better as Martagan and Swann went into action.

She was lightning fast—and deadly, moving with grim economy of movement and absolute body control. The three men in front of her didn't stand a chance. She pulled one of the blades out of the throat of my victim even as he slumped, and rammed it up under the chin of one of hers, then using the handle as a bracing point, ran up the man's corpse and launched herself at the two men beside him. They were dead before her feet touched the marbled floor again.

And then it was five and Swann was using the incredible strength of his exospine to crush the life out of two men at once.

Less than five seconds had passed since Fate had died.

We didn't have time to think about it. We didn't have any kind of fancy plan. The three of us left standing had come in here expecting to make a play for Aldus Keyes and were relying on our contact from Akachi to get us out of there. Without Keyes, we had nothing to barter with.

Fate had well and truly dicked us.

Even so, we couldn't leave him in here and let them turn him into one of those Sleepers. I wouldn't wish that on my worst enemy. So, while Martagan and Swann finished clearing the room, I gathered our erstwhile leader into my arms and figured our best bet was to walk out the front door. After all, our credentials were all good. We were meant to be here.

We'd worry about what happened next assuming we got out of here.

PART THREE

TWIST OF FATE

And that's how we got here, a cemetery in the heart of GenX territory, a red dot in the center of my chest, the rest of my crew dead.

Okay, I'll admit, I've been a little economical with the truth. That's not *exactly* how it is. I mean it is. Obviously, I wouldn't lie to you, but hanging around with Fate all these years has made me one cautious son of a bitch. You don't walk into a situation blind. That's stupid. The truth is I'd thought long and hard about coming here. I'd carried Fate out of that place with my bare hands, I'd said my goodbyes when it mattered. This, the rest of it, was all window dressing. I'd decided to make a pilgrimage back to where it all began, where we first met, and raise a glass to the old bastard, but that would have to wait. Right now there were more pressing things on my mind, like dying all over again.

It really was a last-minute thing to turn up in person, but I wasn't the guy beneath the boughs of the weeping willow in the shadows of the old crematorium furnace. Well, I was, in so much as it looked like me. The shadows helped complete the illusion, meaning no one would see through the hologram. I'd had a bad feeling about this since the moment Swann told me it was happening. The crew gathering so close to GenX, and so soon after the botched blackmail attempt, was just asking for trouble, so I'd taken precautions. If I'm running a hit I like to be in place three hours before things are meant to go down, so figuring other people think the same way, I decided I'd get there three hours before the earliest arrival, meaning I'd been in place before dawn to bury the holographic projector and test the distances on the remote trigger. It was good for four hundred meters. In a cramped, overcrowded, stinking metropolis that was half a world away. I wasn't dressed like a Bleeder, either. I was invisible. Not literally. I was wrapped in the layers of invisibility that the filthy coats upon coats held together by the dirt so deeply ingrained in them that being one of the city's disenfranchised conferred. I looked like a tramp. No one bothered with the homeless. They were just there to be ignored. It had all started when the city had cut off water to one hundred and fifty thousand people's homes, then cut the power, driving them out because the corporations wanted to build more hi-tech facilities and needed the land those houses were built on. They weren't lucky enough to be able to fight back. One thing I've learned since my family was turfed out; it's impossible to fight back from the outside. You need to be on the inside, or you're nothing.

That's my secret. My back story. The stuff no one knows about me. Well. Not no one anymore.

I remembered Fate had used that hologram device back in Akachi, so I made a detour on the way here, hitting his pad on thirty-second floor of the Wan Chai plaza to scavenge a few death goods. I figured I was owed. I'd snagged a few of his other more interesting toys, too. It was a pity to let them go to waste. It was weird being in there on my own, especially because nothing had changed. There were still take-out cartons in the trash. An upscale sushi and sashimi joint from across the plaza famous for exotic takes on traditional Japanese recipes. Expensive. I remember thinking that at least his last meal had been an extravagant one.

Turns out I was right to be suspicious. I looked down at the screen in my hands, which was running a feed from a couple of cameras I'd set up around the cemetery, enabling me to check for heat sources and identify the players GenX had sent in to end us once and for all. I was banking on the fact that cutting the power to the hologram would make it look like I'd fallen to their bullets and that they wouldn't come to check the deed was indeed done. The red dot in the center of my doppelgänger's chest didn't waver.

I smiled as they killed me.

It was a peculiar experience watching myself being taken out.

I watched the clean-up from my hiding place. It was sloppy. And I was half-right, they didn't worry about checking if I was actually dead, but they did check the others, kind of. They bundled Swann on top of Lisl Martagan in Fate's open grave and shoveled the dirt back in on top of them. They came looking for me, of course, and saw the thick trail of blood I'd laid down that morning. It wasn't perfect, but the blood was real, and genetic testing would prove it was mine. I'd been tapping my veins every day since we'd escaped GenX. What can I say, I'm one tricky bastard, too. And it's a good thing I am because their point man did indeed check the blood to confirm my identity. Maybe they weren't completely hopeless amateurs after all.

I'd made sure there was enough blood that even a grunt would be able to tell the wounds were fatal.

But that wasn't enough.

Without a body, they'd never fall for the gag.

I needed them to believe I was dead.

About thirty seconds ago, Marco Guerra had become a ghost.

So, they followed the blood to the next part of my illusion.

It's all about misdirection, giving people visual confirmation of what they already believe. They thought I was dying, too weak to flee on foot, clinging on to consciousness before the big sleep. But I needed it to end without access to my corpse. And that meant going out with a bang.

I'd hacked my way into the computer system controlling my car; it's not difficult to do. People assume these little personal computers that run our lives are so sophisticated, but in reality, the only thing they're really interested in is feeding raw data back to the corporations about our driving habits, our eating habits, places we go, how long we stay, that kind of thing. It seems innocuous enough, it's just metadata after all, but think of it this way: you drive to the docs, then your phone call is to a number registered to a clinic that specializes in abortion, and bingo, the corps know to hit you with all sorts of targeted ads as you move through the city depending on which lobby has fronted up the most cash you'll be bombarded with pro-life stuff or pro-choice, you'll see happy families and ads for diapers and formula or you'll see glimpses of a better life with none of that stuff in. So, once I was in, it wasn't difficult to rig it, so I had a remote control and a C4 under the hood. All I had to do was drive the corpse I'd prepared earlier into the cemetery wall and press the big, red, shiny button to blow the thing sky high and bingo, they'd got the crispy-fried corpse they wanted, with DNA proof it was me inside that burning wreck.

They watched me burn.

They didn't check it was me inside there.

Why would they?

And just like that, I was a ghost.

Or, more accurately: just like that, I was a revenant.

Because I was going to avenge my crew.

I waited a long time before I broke cover.

Patience is a bitch, but you need it in this business. A lot of it can be simply sitting and waiting for the shit to hit the fan.

I couldn't go home. I couldn't hit any of the joints the old crew would normally be seen, not if I wanted to stay dead without actually winding up six feet under. I needed a bolt hole. In this case, a bolt hole that wasn't five star, didn't have room service and corruptible maître d'hôtel's willing to sell me out to the highest bidder. Not that any respectable establishment would have let me in dressed like this. No, I needed to take a walk on the seedy side of life. Go places I wouldn't be recognized. Buy myself some time through anonymity. I'm not proud. I don't need the finer things in life to feel complete. A full belly is about all I need. I needed to be clever. I couldn't risk using any of my old—and very traceable—sources of finance, either. No credit card spending. From now on in it had to be all cash all the time. Nothing that could be traced back to Marco Guerra.

One thing I knew for certain, though: I couldn't do this alone. I couldn't go up against GenX by myself. One man can't bring down a global corporation the size of that monstrosity. It's just not doable. With a global population upwards of sixteen billion during the last census in 2150, we're talking about eight billion workers out there, probably one billion of them in the pocket of GenX. One billion people. We're also talking about a lot of hungry people without steady income who'd do pretty much anything for a sniff of the almighty dollar. You can't hide from that. Not for any length of time. Not if they've actively labeled you public enemy number one. I needed to put a new crew together, but I couldn't use the one thing I had going for me: my reputation.

Sometimes it sucks to be me.

But I'd still rather that than be Swann, Martagan or Fate right now.

So I found a low rent flea pit on the edge of the vast sprawl. It offered basic net facilities, nothing fancy, but meant I could jack into the system and put out feelers, see if there were any names out there I recognized looking for work.

The first one I found was Rowel Gant.

Gant is a hard ass. He's the kind of man you want at your side if you plan on walking into Hell to take out the Dark Lord himself. He's the only man on earth the Devil is pissing himself about facing down in those fiery pits when he finally passes on. I found him in bed with a couple of Desi whores in New Delhi. He wasn't pleased to see me. It *was* a gun in his pocket.

I'd only met Gant a couple of times in my life. Both times we'd come up against each other on other sides of a gig. Both times I'd come away feeling very lucky to be alive. I had three scars thanks to him. One of them split me from stem to stern. That I walked away from it was a miracle and in no small part down to the fact that Swann was every bit as crazy as Gant.

"You look in bad shape for a dead man," Gant said, muzzle of his AC 17 aimed squarely at my balls. I felt them shrink up inside me.

I scratched at what had become my scruffy grey beard. "We need to talk."

"I don't think so. Talking to you is liable to get me killed."

"True. But I don't know who else to turn to. I'm putting together a new crew."

"Why the fuck would you want to do that?"

"I'm moving into the revenge business."

"Makes sense, I suppose. You're not content with being alive, so you're going out of your way to make sure you end up dead all over again."

"Something like that. We were set up. My team was murdered. You wouldn't take that if it was your crew."

"No. But then, I'd probably be the one who murdered them." He wasn't joking. He was a very disturbed man. Which was exactly what I needed right then. "How much you offering?"

"I've got some cash stashed from before, but the minute I try and lay my hands on it it's going to set off all sorts of alarms, and everyone will know I'm still alive."

"How much are we talking?"

"A couple of million, give or take, plus assets."

"My, my, you boys really were big business at the end, eh? I'll take it."

"I wasn't offering it."

"I know. But you're dead. I'll take it anyway. It's just easier if you agree first. Let me worry about how I get my hands on it. Consider it my signing on bonus."

I nodded. What else could I do? I needed him, and he knew it.

"I'd have done it for nothing, you know?" Gant said, a couple of days later. "I've always fancied a suicide run against one of the big corps. Blaze of glory shit, you know the kind of thing?"

"Now you tell me," I said.

We'd got a lead on a Flatliner who was in deep shit with GenX and looking for a lifeline.

I wasn't above pretending we had a chance if it meant we were one step closer to assembling the dream team.

I thought I was living rough. Mel Kamahi had taken it to a whole new level of desperation. She wasn't pleased to see us. She hadn't always been a Flatliner. She'd spent most of her life as a hacker, specializing on the kinds of things likely to get you a very long stretch in a deep, dark, technology-less hole. Her big score had been a hit on Warwulf-Blaze where she'd cleaned out a couple of the commodity broker's key accounts and made a few very rich friends even richer. Not that they were mathematically inclined to count exactly how many zeroes she added to their already obscene bank balances. It nearly took the corp under, it was that audacious. Of course, it had been an inside job. She'd wormed her way into every nook and corporate cranny laying down a plan to make out like a bandit, crafting a dozen flawless identities she could sell out one by one to misdirect Warwulf-Blaze from the actual crime at hand. She was clever. I like clever people. They're exactly what you need in your corner.

In point of fact, she was clever enough to know the ghost and the madman were on their way long before we turned up at her door.

She also had a piece of information that, all things considered, was priceless.

Of course, I didn't believe her when she told me. Not at first. I made her prove it. When she did, I knew there was no way I was going anywhere without her as my intel gather. That woman has mad skills.

The information?

It was dusk on the third day. I think it was the third day. It could have been the fourth. Or even the fifth. They all blurred together. I hadn't slept in I don't know how long. Since she'd told me, I guess. I didn't want to believe. I refused to.

But Randall Fate was a creature of habit, even when he was dead.

Even when I saw him with my own two eyes, I couldn't quite believe it. I'd carried him out of there. I'd buried him. Or at least I'd buried someone. Because Randall Fate was very much alive and well and living in Old Tokyo. He didn't even have the decency to move. He had taken up residence in the Wan Chai tower again. At first, he was simply a thermal blur through the scope, moving about the room while I surveilled it from a safe distance across in the belfry of the super church across the plaza. I felt like a voyeur spying on my old life. For the first few hours, I refused to believe it was really him, but ghosts didn't give off heat signatures. Had it been a big old cold spot, maybe, but the signal I was picking up was unmistakably warm-blooded.

Even with the intense magnification of the sniper rifle's telescopic lens, the tint on the tower's glass meant I couldn't get a clear sight of the man—not clear enough to identify him beyond a lens-flare of doubt. Not at first. And as tempting as it was to pull the trigger, I knew full well the toughened glass between us was thick enough to stop anything my Zamtech could send its way. Maybe a Predator KVK might penetrate it, but even that was a maybe. Fate was paranoid. Paranoid men didn't leave themselves open to stray bullets. They took precautions.

My head was buzzing.

Was it really him?

How could it be really him?

But if it was... did that mean he'd sold us out?

It had to.

No matter what I thought I'd seen with my own eyes... no matter the grief I'd felt carrying him out of there... Fate had engineered the whole thing. Somehow. Despite Fate's miraculous resurrection, my crew was dead. That wasn't changing. Because that man in there wasn't the Randall Fate I knew. He wasn't the man who had mentored us. He wasn't our friend. He was just the son of a bitch who had sold us out to save his own skin. When he'd come to me pitching the job he'd promised, it would make us richer than god. I guess that meant the payoff he'd engineered for himself made him richer than four gods, never mind one.

Money.

Was it really that simple?

Of course it was.

Fate lived, ate and breathed money.

It was his Alpha and Omega.

The game had just changed.

Big time.

Now I wasn't going up against some faceless corporate masters.

It was personal.

This was between me and Fate.

I wanted to know how he'd done it, of course.

How was almost more important than why, right now.

It wasn't like I'd carried a hologram out of GenX.

He didn't know I knew he was alive. But I was regretting my visit to the apartment before the funeral to stock up. If he went through his gear, he'd know stuff was missing. If he went through the security records, he'd work out my key had activated the locks. So that was the first thing I needed Mel to fix. And fast. She needed to wipe any trace of me in that place. She thought it would be fun to make it look as though Fate's own biometric key had been used to open the door, meaning he'd seemingly robbed himself. I thought it was a bit cute, but I was quite happy for him to waste time worrying about who his quantum burglar was while I got on with the serious business of plotting out a very personal, very brutal revenge for my friends.

And I'll be honest, even confronted with the truth, I couldn't actually believe it.

I let Mel get on with covering my tracks and went in search of the final member of my team.

An assassin.

I knew who I wanted, but all I had was a name: Tenebrae.

There's something mildly amusing about a ghost chasing a shadow...

But then, I've always had a perverse sense of humor.

How do you arrange a meeting with a hitman?

Easy.

Hire him to kill you.

I put the word out there was a new Bleeder in town, a ghost, and that I wanted his spectral head on a platter. There were plenty of takers, of course, from inexperienced wannabes with big ideas about their so-called talents to some seriously dangerous souls. I was only interested in one of them, but Tenebrae himself didn't bite. Two weeks after the massacre at Fate's funeral a broker reached out. The message came through coded, requesting a sit-down. The venue was a seedy old joint in the heart of the red-light district in Old Tokyo. Outside were neon lights for LIVE GIRLS, for GIRLS GIRLS GIRLS and guaranteed LIVE SEX while barkers that promised everything from ping pong shows to smoking genitalia and, well, everything imaginable. You name the perversion, someone along that strip was willing to feed it for cash. Not my ideal choice, but it offered a layer of anonymity, so it worked.

Inside, I felt like I'd just walked into the Stripper's Graveyard where old pole dancers came to die. I ordered an overpriced shot of single malt, no ice and sat in a private booth to wait for my contact to show.

I was served by a girl young enough to be my daughter, and attractive enough for me to be glad she wasn't.

The lights were low, blacking out everything bar the stage area, where a geriatric stripper leaned on her Zimmer and wiggled her ass suggestively. Okay, it wasn't *quite* that bad, but I could see the extra roll of fat around her liposuction scars and the stretch marks where her sagging breasts hung low. Not even the tassels could save them. Her body was like a lunar landscape, all pitted and craggy. The music–supplied by a coin-fed jukebox in the corner–was about as inappropriately sexy as it could possibly have been. It was the very definition of unpleasant juxtaposition. The stripper gyrated her hips gamely, slipping her thumbs beneath the straps her thong and started to ease it down. I really didn't want to see what happened next, so I turned to the rest of the room, scanning the dark for half-lit faces, but the booths were all carefully arranged to preserve clientele anonymity.

I checked my watch. Time was ticking by. There was no sign of the broker. Or maybe there was. I didn't know who I was supposed to meet. I wasn't sure how long I was prepared to wait.

Someone else fed the jukebox. The singer could hardly have imagined a darker interpretation of their lyrics than the one being danced on the stage right now if they'd tried. It wasn't so much ironic as it was prophetic. After a few minutes of unbearable grinding, the strippers on stage switched. The new one was no more appealing than the last one, her Caesarean scar looking like a botched Frankensteinian transplant.

I was going to have to wash my mind out with bleach when I got home.

The broker obviously had a twisted sense of humor.

I checked my watch again then gestured one of the waitresses over. She flashed me a fifty-buck smile – the going rate for the single shot she thought I was going to order – and leaned in close, making sure I got an eyeful of her ample cleavage as she took my order.

"I'm looking for someone," I said.

She looked at me blankly.

I tried again, "I'm looking for someone? I'm supposed to meet them here."

Misunderstanding, the waitress waved over one of the past-their-sell-by-date strippers leaning against the back wall, thinking I wanted a table dance.

I held up my hands, shaking my head, "No, no. I didn't mean—" my face twisted. "I'm supposed to meet someone here. I don't know their name."

"Sorry, man, no singles here tonight. There's a dike couple if that's your thing," She shrugged, tilting her head toward another booth. "But they're busy sucking face. Can I get you another drink? Single malt, right? The good stuff."

The music changed again.

I dreaded to think what was happening on the stage and shifted in my seat so I didn't have to find out. I decided to give it another hour before heading home. "Why not?" I said, "But make it a double. I think I'm going to need it if I want to sleep tonight."

She laughed, but it was the kind of perfunctory, half-hearted laugh that meant she was working her ass off for that tip and she wanted me to know it.

I drank.

I waited.

I turned down a double-team table dance, one of the pair dressed in weird tin-foil silver spandex, the other in some sort of furry costume. Not my scene. In the background, the jukebox offered an unusual array of noise. The broker didn't show.

I wasn't about to stick around until the lights came up—I definitely didn't want to see what the girls looked like in the cold light of day. I removed a fifty from my wallet, folded it up and left it underneath the tumbler before heading for the door, figuring it had been an expensive waste of time.

It wasn't.

The broker met me as I stepped out into the street. "Hope you enjoyed the show, Mister Guerra."

The cold air hit me like a slap across the face, his use of my name like a kick in the balls. So much for being a ghost.

It was three in the morning, and there wasn't a soul in sight.

The club's neon sign sizzled and hummed behind us.

"Honestly, I could have lived without it," I said.

"Shall we walk awhile?"

"Well I'm not going back in there, so yes."

We walked a while in silence, then he said, "My factor is most interested as to why you would want to kill yourself and pay so handsomely in the process? She suggested pills or a razor blade if you are averse to blowing your brains out. She is, of course, happy to take the contract assuming you are quite determined to die. You need only nod once, now, and we'll consider the deal done."

"Ah," I said. "No," I said.

"Then why, she would like to know, have you been so careless?"

That threw me.

"What do you mean?"

I thought I'd been clever. I'd not returned to any of the old haunts. I'd stayed out of the Beetle dens and everything else that might have brought the attention of my old employers.

He grabbed my wrists and dragged me to the side of the road. I was about to wrench my hand free and hammer my fist into the center of his face—I don't think I've mentioned it before, but I've got a real aversion to people touching me—but before I could, he'd twisted them palms up and with a tiny razor embedded in his thumb cut an inch long scar in the synth skin. Blood bubbled up. He pressed deep, and a tiny electronic tracking device emerged.

Sometimes I really am a fucking idiot.

Fate had chipped me. Or at least paid off some friendly doc to do it after the Akachi job, so he had eyes and ears on me at all times.

I felt sick.

He knew I was alive.

He'd known all the time.

I was burned. I couldn't go back to the bolt hole, they'd have it under surveillance. I needed to warn Gant to get out of there and take evasive measures. I had no doubt he could look after himself, but there was no way we could meet up if he were being followed otherwise the broker's impromptu surgery would be for nothing.

The broker palmed the tracker. "Let me take care of this for you," he said. He wasn't doing it out of any form of generosity. He intended to use it to lead Randall Fate a merry dance for his assassin. Good for him.

"Now that we've established you have no intention of suicide, and that someone has been following you for quite some time, why the rouse? I don't mind admitting we are most curious. The loss of your crew sent shockwaves through the community. But there are whispers... things might not be all that they seem?"

"That's one way of putting it," I said.

"Care to expand?"

"Can I rely on your discretion?"

"Bought and paid for," he assured me. "Or it will be, assuming we take whatever job it is you really want to hire Tenebrae for."

"We were betrayed." He waited for me to go on. "By one of our own." Again nothing. He knew how to get answers with silence. That was an impressive skill. "Fate's alive. He faked his own death."

"Ah, so this is about revenge?"

"Plain and simple. He sold us out to the corp, got my friends killed to save his own skin and make a few bucks in the process. He's going to pay for that."

"Who else have you got on your side?"

"A Flatliner, Mel Kamahi, and Rowel Gant."

"I know them. Good at what they do. As are you. With Tenebrae, you would make quite a team. And you have a plan?"

"Right now I'm improvising," I admitted.

"Not ideal."

"Perhaps not, but I've only known that Fate is still alive for a few days. Up until then, I'd been planning to go up against GenX all by myself."

"Well I can't fault you're bravery, Mister Guerra. Not, perhaps, the wisest course of action, though."

"I worked that out for myself."

"Very well, I will take your proposition back to her. I cannot guarantee she will accept it, but I will advise her to take it under consideration. In the meantime, I suggest you get some sleep. Tomorrow promises to be a long day."

He wasn't wrong.

Some days feel like they're packed with a lot more than twenty-four hours.

This was one of them.

I ordered a strong black coffee thick enough to stand the spoon up in and leaned against the battered metal counter of the vendor's food cart. Street food was the lifeblood of the megacities these days. Always people crowding around them. Bright lights above them enticing the hungry, the restless, the poor. Security would move them on after a while so you never knew where you'd find them again on their rotation through dozens of good spots they knew would keep the money coming. The coffee was good. I was on my own and for the first time since the meeting with the broker not jumping at shadows.

I slid a couple of crumpled notes across the counter in return for a stew pot of noodles and mixed mystery meats. I probably would have been better off with faux-fish bagel or something, but I've got an adventurous palate and the constitution to match. I tucked in with my chopsticks.

I didn't notice the woman slide onto the stool beside me until she spoke. "What's good here?"

"Nothing," I said, turning to face her.

She was black—properly ebon, a Nubian goddess of a woman, with a long graceful black swan's neck and deep soulful eyes that were almost as dark as her skin. She smiled. I understood exactly why the region her genetic roots stemmed from was known as the Cradle of Life in that one fleeting moment. Who wouldn't want to create life, or at least practice, with those genes?

"Pity," she said. "My friend tells me you're looking to put together a team, at least temporarily?"

I looked at her.

Black as night.

Tenebrae. It couldn't be anyone else. Funny when you don't know what to expect, you'd think you couldn't be surprised by the reality, but I was.

"Are you interested?"

"Well I wasn't thinking of anything beyond lunch," she said. Funny lady.

"Not into commitment?"

"Not a big fan of being tied down, no," the way she said it was deliberately flirtatious. I didn't rise to the bait. On another day, absolutely, I'm not above a little double entendre. I focussed on the noodle dangling from the end of my chopsticks and slurped it up. I washed it down with a swig of coffee then said, "Well, if you're in, you're all in. If you can't do that, I'll find someone else. I don't have time for games."

"But they won't be as good as me," she promised.

She was right, of course. If her reputation was anything to go by there was no one quite like her out there. But then my reputation was pretty damn good, and any idiot could have looked at the mess I was in and realized just how fucked I was, and how little my carefully cultivated reputation was going to help. Traffic moved around us, the constant ebb and flow of the jammed up city. Pedestrians walked in their little huddles, a few walked alone, eyes on some distant prize and moving with purpose. Everyone had a purpose. The corporations gave them one. I'd had one of those. Now I had something different. It wasn't exactly a purpose. It transcended that into... into what? An obsession?

"All I need is someone willing to die for the cause."

"How very noble, but surely it's better to find someone good enough to stay alive for the cause?"

"You know what we're going up against, do you really think anyone will be left standing at the end of it?"

"If they're good enough," she said, and it was obvious she meant it. And I'll admit, I was buying into it.

"So, are you in?"

"Answer me this first: have you worked out how he did it?"

I didn't need to ask who he was, or what it was he did. It was the same question I'd been asking myself for days: how did Fate fool me into thinking he was dead?

"No," I admitted.

"Then I'm in."

That surprised me. I don't know what I'd expected, to be mocked, maybe, for my gullibility, or my complicit naïveté. I didn't expect it to be what she wanted to hear. Turns out she was big on truth, and the fact I owned up to my own shortcomings was exactly what the assassin wanted to hear.

I had my team.

"What do you know about what happened?" Tenebrae asked.

"I told you."

"Tell me again."

"He took an arc-blade to the gut. It opened him up. He died. I carried him out of there in my arms. He was dead."

"Well, obviously he wasn't. So the only two things you know for sure are he took a blade, and you carried him out of trouble. So the blade has to be your answer."

"I'm not sure I follow," I admitted.

"I do," Gant said. "You know he wasn't dead, you've got proof now, but something happened between him being stabbed and you carrying him out that convinced you he was dead."

"Exactly," the assassin agreed.

I'd run events over in my mind a thousand times. More. But they were always the same. I wasn't seeing it. Maybe my subconscious was working away on it, linking the bits of the puzzle without me realizing what was going on, but my surface mind was clueless. Certain key factors kept coming into sharp focus: Fate had instigated it. I realized that now. He'd been the one who'd lost his cool and killed Auster, damning the rest of us. He didn't have to do that. He'd deliberately escalated things with a shocking level of violence. We're violent people, but it has its place. That room wasn't it, even with all of the Sleepers surrounding us. I'd assumed he thought he was cutting off their heads, metaphorically speaking. But it was more than that. He'd given a signal to someone he'd paid off inside GenX, surely? One of the goons who'd escorted us down there. Probably the one who'd put the arc-blade through his spine after he'd shot Auster. That made sense. That was a deduction I could get behind. He'd needed us to know he was dead. To see it not just hear about it. He needed one of us to carry him out of there. But how do you arrange something like that? He could risk stopping his heart for that long, surely? There was no guarantee how quickly we could get out of there, and as any Flatliner will tell you, those precious few seconds, they're fine margins you don't want to fuck with.

"So how did he do it?"

"He couldn't be dead, we agree on that, right?"

I nodded.

"So he had to be alive."

She was saying the same thing, surely?

I nodded again.

"His heart was beating, either so slowly or so faintly you failed to notice and mistook him for dead." That made sense. "And," she continued, "For that to happen he needed to be in precise control of his apparent death. He couldn't risk the blade going in an inch too high and actually piercing the heart, but he needed it to seem as if it had punctured something vital and die quickly." I was nodding again. "So it couldn't be the blade that did the work, it was purely the method of delivery."

"Poison," I said, catching on. "Something that would slow the heart without actually killing him."

Tenebrae nodded, "Now you're getting there."

"What can do that?"

She smiled. "Fugu."

I resisted the temptation to say fugu, too. I'd heard the word before. You couldn't avoid it if you spent any time living in Old Tokyo. Fugu. Pufferfish. A delicacy as likely to kill you as sate your hunger. Over a thousand times more toxic than cyanide, the fish's vital organs are infused with enough Tetrodotoxin, a bacterial neurotoxin, to kill thirty people. But, in the hands of someone who knows what they're doing, exposure doesn't have to mean death. There's an alternative. The fugu poison will basically zombify you, taking out higher brain function and slowing the heart rate to a point that the beating is virtually undetectable with more than a minute between each.

She'd piqued my interest. It made sense.

I turned to Mel Kamahi. "I want you to do something for me."

"You're the boss," she said.

"Hack into the security at Fate's Wan Chai plaza."

"What am I looking for?"

I was remembering something I'd seen when I'd broken in to steal the holographic projector and a few other goodies, tossed away in the trash: those expensive take-out boxes from the luxury sushi and sashimi place. One of the specialties of that place was Takifugu. Fugu.

"Go through surveillance footage for the twenty-four hours before he died. Find out what he had for his last meal."

⌖

I was right.

Mel came back to us about twenty minutes later with everything we could have possibly wanted to know about Randall Fate's final hours—at least the ones he'd spent within the luxury apartments in the Wan Chai super tower. "He ordered sashimi from Kyūbey, kaiseki, delivered to the apartment but switched out the Bluefin for Takifugu. He also requested the offal and paid a premium for it." I nodded. The restaurants weren't supposed to sell that sort of stuff, but Fate talked best with money. He could be very persuasive with the almighty dollar in his hand. The offal accounted for how he could be sure the fish would contain the Tetrodotoxin he needed. It was the smoking gun I'd been looking for, and it had been staring me in the face for weeks, I just hadn't known that all I needed to do was root around in the real trash, I'd been too busy rooting around in the metaphorical trash of Fate's life. "It gets better," she promised and triggered a video loop on the small screen rig she'd put on the counter between us.

Gant and Tenebrae moved in closer so they could see what was going on.

The angle was strange; the surveillance camera distorted the dimensions of the room, making Fate seem taller than he was. I watched my old mentor—my friend—go to the door and collect his meal from the delivery boy, trading him an overly generous tip for the three boxes of food. Two he took to the counter and dished up, the finely sliced Takifugu sashimi and rice. The third he set aside. She fast-forwarded through him eating and the general minutia of his life until the moment he opened his weapon cupboard and selected an arc-blade, which he carried reverently across to the counter where the third box had remained untouched.

Fate put on a pair of thin surgical gloves before he opened the box, and even then he did so carefully.

Inside were two small discs of meat.

It took me a second to work out what they were.

He actually looked up at the camera then, and smiled, like he knew I was watching.

You bastard, I thought, as he took one between forefinger and thumb and ran it slowly and carefully down the length of the arc-blade, then took the other and repeated the motion down the other side of the blade. I didn't know much about fugu, save for the fact that the build-up of toxins inside the fish was concentrated in its skin, liver, testicles, and ovaries. Fate put the pufferfish's testicles back in the box and tossed them in the trash.

"And there you have it," Mel said. "An imprecise science at best, a massive risk at worst, but that's how he fooled you all."

And that's why Martagan and Swann were dead: a bastard rubbing a couple of fish testicles on a blade.

"I guess that pretty much kills any benefit of the doubt I might have wanted to afford him," I said. Right up until that moment, seeing him prepare the poisoned blade, I hadn't wanted to believe he was actually capable of betraying us all. Part of me had been praying that Mel would turn up proof that it was all a terrible mistake, and that Fate was actually at the bottom of that hole with Martagan and Swann. That would have been better. But like the old song says, you can't always get what you want.

I hope he was really well paid for it, that's all I can say.

It wouldn't help him.

He might be richer than god, but I was more wrathful.

All things considered, I almost pitied him.

PART FOUR

TEMPTED FATE

I'd known Fate for most of my adult life. At times I joked that I knew him better than I knew myself. I was wrong, obviously. He still had the capacity to surprise me, but did I have what it took to surprise him?

A confidence trick exploits basic characteristics of the human psyche: dishonesty, honesty, vanity, compassion, credulity, irresponsibility, naïveté, or greed. One of them, all of them, or some of them together. It depended on the mark. There were two ways it could work, but both came down to the same thing, getting the mark to trust us. Not necessarily the easiest, but the best way, was to get Fate to trust us by giving him our confidence. Exposing ourselves to him. Or at least making him think we were doing that. That meant he needed to believe we were trustworthy.

What did I know about Randall Fate?

I knew what he liked, and what he didn't.

But more importantly, I knew what he couldn't resist.

For one thing, he had a predilection for unconventional beauty.

That was the kind of detail you needed to know if you were going to bait a honey trap.

I wasn't sure Tenebrae's Nubian physique and hard polished ebony lines would do it for him, but he was a man, and she was what I had to work with. Plus, I'll be absolutely dead straight, I couldn't imagine anyone saying no to her—and not because of her exotic looks, but purely because of the force of her personality. The woman oozed power and confidence, two huge aphrodisiacs in my line of work, but it was the grace with which she moved that was absolutely contagious. So I had faith. But we had to do this without Fate working out I was the one pulling the strings in the background. That meant being clever. And given the fact that he'd had me chipped, one of us was decidedly more savvy than the other. I was banking on him not knowing that Tenebrae's broker had paid a street urchin good cash to have the chip implanted subcutaneously, and then told to keep moving about the city to spread a false trail for me. The watcher becomes the watched and all that.

The best way to lure Fate out was a double whammy, hit him with the full package, the sex and the money. Present an opportunity that promised lots of both, and hope the fish took the hook. That would mean Mel needed to make our assassin credible, sorting out credentials that couldn't be easily broken, and setting up Gant as her muscle. Given the color of her skin, Akachi was the obvious corporation, but we couldn't go with the obvious because we couldn't be sure Fate didn't have a man inside there. There were too many suppositions for my liking, but I wasn't a conman by nature. I'd heard the catchphrases, of course: ABC, Always Be Conning, and my favorite, win at all costs, lose if it helps you win, and always, always, cheat.

We were going to need a lot of stuff for this to work. Right now all we had was the mark. We needed a lot more than that. There are six stages to a con, the first, the foundation. You need to lay the groundwork, which is what we were doing now. Get things in place. To hook Fate, we were going to need to play to three core traits: his dishonesty, his vanity, and his greed. We couldn't do anything until we had all that in place.

"We're going to need your broker as a go-between," I said to

Tenebrae. "Do you think he'll be up for the role?"

"Absolutely. He likes to get his hands dirty."

"Good. We're going to need a place. Somewhere ostentatious. Luxurious. The kind Fate would dream of, you know?"

She nodded. "Leave it with me. What else do we need?"

I gave her a list.

This is how a good con works:

After you've laid the foundations, the next stage of a con is the approach, which has to be the riskiest part of it. Get it wrong, and you're blown out of the water. We couldn't set it up so that Tenebrae just plunked herself down beside Fate in a bar and randomly started hitting on him. He wouldn't buy that. It needed to look more... coincidental... like it was ideal. That would take some planning.

Then there's the build-up, which is where we'd need to stir up Fate's curiosity, get him interested in what we were selling. That was the part where I was relying on his vanity to kick in, not just greed. Sure the offer of profit would be there, and obvious, but you can make money on any gig. To be sure of hooking him, we needed him to believe we were talking about something next-to-impossible. Something only the best of the best could pull off, hence why we'd gone looking for him. Then that burning greed and his blazing vanity together would be enough to warp his judgment. I needed him to make some bad decisions—to be honest, the same kind of bad decisions he'd been making over the last year or so. I was banking on them not being part of a long con of his own, but rather a difficult-to-break pattern of behavior.

Next comes the convincer, the pay-off, where we let him think he's winning. Money works. A few small wins to play on both greed and gullibility. The whole objective here is to get rid of any lingering doubts he might have. We needed him all in, so if we had to pay for the privilege, so be it, it'd be money well spent.

Which opens up the Hurrah. No decent con is complete without a grand spanner in the works; a sudden crisis that turns up just at the right moment to push the mark over the last hurdle and give him no choice but to dive all in. Then it's all about good faith, as the con you're in absolute control for the In-and-In, the end-game where you fleece the mark for everything he's got.

Of course, you couldn't do it alone—at least not well. Especially not the plan I had in mind, which was going to take corroboration. Fate was many things, but he wasn't gullible. That's where the assassin's broker would come in. He was our external validation.

There are as many cons and variants of cons as there are conmen. Some, like the Spanish Prisoner, were as old as the hills and had been through dozens of iterations over the years, adapting to the times. Others play on romance, like the Sweetheart Deal, which preyed on the lovelorn with the ultimate promise of marriage as the prize, the 'sweetheart' stuck in her own country, victim of the vile corporation, and needs cash to get out. It's obvious, and it's sad, but people still fall for it because they want to believe in love. They almost deserve to be scammed, like the horny little souls who fall for the Badger Game. What is it they say about a fool and his money? Lure the mark into a compromising position, be it boys, girls, or a little half-n-half, whatever their proclivity, and then blackmail them.

I'd done my research.

There's nothing like being thorough. That was part of the foundation. The truth was there were countless cons, bait and switch, pigeon drops, flim-flams, rip deals and jam auctions and stuff that until a few days ago had meant nothing to me. None of them would work out of the box. Not with Fate. They'd need to be massaged into a workable con, and even then the risk was he'd see us coming and try to turn it around on us, to make the conners the conned.

In fact, I was banking on it.

It was time to play.

Tenebrae's broker, a man called Imsen, worked hard on the procurement, actually managing to secure us the penthouse on a Dubai super tower owned by Ayako-Mizuki, and then furnishing it as the ultimate Gene Sculpt Clinic. There are plenty of those about, of course, but nothing quite like what we were selling. We needed staffers of course, and a doc who knew what he was talking about, which all took money, but that we had in spades thanks to the fact Gant had cleaned out all of my 'dead man's accounts.'

Basically what we were doing was setting up what con artists would call a 'Big Shop'—it had to be believable, and stand up to more than just a surface-scratching inspection.

It was and it would.

Now it was all about his vanity.

Imsen set up a meet with Tenebrae. The meet was in a controlled environment. We had surveillance in place so I could watch it all, and Gant was on hand to crush Fate if things got out of hand.

It would have been easy to just kill him there and then once we'd drawn him out of the woodwork, but that wasn't enough. It needed to be a fate worse than death. Anything else and he was getting off too easily. But I'll admit I was tempted to just put a bullet in his head and be done with it.

The broker sat down at the bar. He had a rolled up newspaper as a prop to identify himself; very old school. No one bought newspapers these days, they had their steady stream of the woes of the world pumped directly into their datasets and rigs and whatever else they used to stay connected. It was quaint. I liked the touch. He unfolded it and waited. We had three cameras covering the angles, watching, and Gant was behind the bar, polishing out an empty—and sparklingly clean—glass with a towel. Behind him, there was a stained glass window of St Jude, patron saints of losers. Sorry, lost causes. Not that there's a big difference.

Fate walked into the bar. It sounds like the beginning of a joke. It wasn't funny. My heartbeat was just a little bit faster. I hadn't seen him since he'd died. Or hadn't died. It was still hard to wrap my head around that. I'd carried him out of there, dosed up on fugu fish toxins. I'd grieved for him. And the fucker had been laughing at me and working out how to spend the cash he'd been paid for turning me over to GenX. I'd thought for a while that it was Akachi looking for payback for the absolute clusterfuck of Africa, but it wasn't. The money came from GenX, just like the half-arsed hit squad that took out Swann and Martagan. Fate was entirely in their pocket. He was a company man through and through.

But he was also one vain, greedy bastard.

He looked around. Old habits die hard. Know your surrounds. Ways in, ways out. Check out how many possible areas of conflict there are inside, where the obvious threats lie. Knowledge is the key to staying alive when you're walking into unknown and possibly hostile territory. Fate identified the broker and crossed the sticky floor to where he sat. Fate sat down beside him without a word. He looked across the bar at Gant, and for a second I was worried I saw a flicker of recognition in his eyes, but he ordered a drink and paid, so whatever he thought he saw, he dismissed.

"How's death working out for you?" the broker said. It was a prearranged signal. It meant they were good to talk freely. Fate had his own pre-agreed answer, "Pushing up daisies is overrated," if it was good, "I'm beginning to fester," if it wasn't.

He didn't say anything for a few seconds, checking out the room again in the backward land of the glass behind the bar.

"Pushing up daisies is overrated," he offered, eventually.

The broker nodded slowly and unfolded his newspaper. There was something inside it, but even with three camera angles, I couldn't get a clear sight.

"I won't waste your time or mine, Mister Fate. I have a proposition for you. I'm hoping it will be of interest. It will certainly be lucrative."

"Speak to me," Fate said.

It was weird hearing his voice again. Not exactly like a ghost, but there was definitely an element of the other side about it in that he'd gone from being a friend to being an enemy.

"It's quite simple, I represent some very wealthy men who are looking to take advantage of some developments in technology you may be familiar with, notably genetic repatterning."

"I'm aware of the concept," Fate conceded, giving nothing away.

"They have procured the services of a willing host," the broker said, "and are willing to offer a lot of money for you to act as the blueprint, taking your skills and memories and transforming an ordinary woman into a super soldier with all of your skills and abilities, Mister Fate."

"Why me?"

"Because they want the best," the broker said, without missing a beat.

"I'm not buying it," Fate said, and my heart stopped beating. It would all fall apart, right there, right then, if he walked out of there without taking the bait. "There are hundreds of Bleeders out there you could have taken this offer to, some better than me, the law of averages says that, a lot of them more desperate than me, so I'll ask you again, why me?"

"And I'll give you the same answer, Mister Fate, because my client wants the best. They are aware of your record. You don't get to live through fifty successful missions without learning a lot about how to live as well as how to die, even if you don't actively recall all of this information you've absorbed from these experiences, it's all still locked away in there. They'd be paying for your successes."

"And the more recent failures?"

"You can learn more from a failed mission," the broker said calmly, "than you can from a dozen successful ones."

He was good. I believed him. But did Fate?

"So what exactly are they buying? I mean what are we talking about? Do they stick a probe in my brain and root around?"

Okay, we'd got his attention. That was the hardest part. Now to reel him in.

The broker smiled. "Nothing quite so barbaric, I assure you. They are very much at the proof of concept stage so they would be offering you twenty million, a one-shot deal, to store your brain patterns on their system."

"Downloading me into the machine?"

"Crudely, I suppose."

"But it doesn't affect me, right? I'm not losing my memories, my skills, nothing like that?"

"No, it's like making a recording. A copy." He resisted saying clone. People still get very tetchy when words like that are bandied about, and given what happened to us in Akachi, we didn't want to overplay our hand. We wanted him to put two and two together and realize—wrongly—where this money was coming from. "That copy will be used to overwrite their guinea pig, giving her all of your memories and unique skills, right down to ingrained muscle memory. In a matter of hours, she will go from a woman they dragged in off the streets into a copy of you, one of the most lethal fighters of the modern age." And to sell the illusion that what we were peddling was real, Tenebrae would put on one hell of a demonstration. I'd feed her with some juicy facts only someone who was there would know, including moves Fate had pulled, and con him into believing he was looking at a living, breathing female version of himself.

What could possibly go wrong?

"And then what?"

"And then, with the concept proved, we create an army of you."

"Twenty mil isn't enough," Fate said, as I knew he would. "I'd be putting myself out of work."

"With twenty million dollars you would never need to work again," the broker countered.

"I don't do it for the money," Fate lied. "But if a corp like Akachi or GenX gets their hands on this, then I'm done. They'd make a thousand me's, all of them every bit as good as I am. There's only one of me. I can't compete. I'd be obsolete. The payoff isn't enough, sorry."

"What would be enough?"

The question hung between them.

Gant put his towel down on the counter and the well-worn tumbler beside it. He needed to make it look like he wasn't listening. Fate would balk if he realized what was going on, and he was suspicious enough as it was. We didn't want to tip him over the edge.

He looked down at his knuckles, then up at St Jude.

"What would be enough?" he repeated.

The broker waited him out, knowing that he was going to produce some astronomical figure out of his arse and expect to be bartered down. That was all part of the game. Give in too easily to his demands, and again, he'd know something was up.

"An island," he said. "Somewhere warm away from the world. Somewhere I can retire to be king."

Our man laughed. "Well that shouldn't be too difficult," he said, his voice laced with sarcasm. "How about an indigenous tribe to worship you as a god, as well?"

"Now you're talking my language," Fate said.

"Thirty million, anything beyond that is a stretch. How you choose to spend it, however, totally down to you. It might pay for a small garbage island out in the Pacific Rim."

"Fifty." Again, the broker laughed. "You want me that badly, you'll pay for what's up here," Fate tapped his temple. "After all, no one else can give you what I can, right? You said it yourself. I'd be a fool to price myself too low. Seventy-five."

"Bargaining doesn't generally work like that, Mister Fate, you reach a compromise, not continue to drive the price up."

"Eighty," Fate said, quite reasonably.

"That is a lot of money," the broker said.

"Hell, let's make it a round one hundred. Call it factoring in inflation for the rest of my life, and I do intend to live for a long time, after all."

"I'm not sure my clients will go to that, but I could, perhaps, convince them to offer various incentives and stagger payments based upon relative success. After all, one hundred million for one derivative of you is extortionate, but perhaps there could be incremental bonuses based upon how many versions of your brain pattern they release into the world?"

"I'm listening."

"Thirty million regardless of success or failure of the procedure, twenty more if and when my clients build their first army of you—an army in this case amounting to one thousand Bleeders."

I could see Fate thinking about it. He could live a pretty rich life on thirty mil, even if they never built a single Bleeder off his template, but that extra twenty would mean he could live like a king. But it wasn't obscene. It wasn't beyond what clever living could bring him in as a Bleeder over the same span of years, if he stayed at the top of the game. Of course, Fate was smart enough to know he couldn't expect to stay at the top of the game for that long. That was the lure. It was like offering him the chance to cash out on a winning bet twenty years early and keep his winnings.

"I'll need to see your operation, of course," Fate said, and I knew the broker had done his job.

The broker made arrangements for Fate's visit to the Dubai super tower and its faux Gene Sculpt Clinic, no expense spared. And again, to plant the seed, the plane's manifest tracked back to Ayako-Mizuki, making it two-for-two with the ownership of the tower. I knew Fate would do his research. He was careful. He wouldn't walk blindly into the place. He'd want to know exactly who he was dealing with on the other side of the broker, even if he was too polite to ask.

I flew the plane from Old Tokyo. I even enjoyed doing the whole buckle-up announcement and wishing him a pleasant flight. I deepened my voice an octave, daring him to recognize me and force his way through the door into the cockpit. He didn't. Or if he did, he didn't act on it, which was the same thing. It was a smooth flight, only a few bumps along the way. We made Dubai in good time. I watched Fate whisked away from the tarmac in a ridiculously expensive limo driven by Rowel Gant, all customs clearances pre-arranged thanks to a few greased palms. Again, that helped serve the illusion that this was all semi-legit corporation business. That was the kind thing the big boys did with their cash to impress people they wanted to own a piece of.

Gant drove fast, seemingly sweeping through the Downtown city with its oil-rich denizens, but actually taking a detour that allowed me to get into place at the super tower before Fate arrived. When he finally delivered Fate to the foot of the enormous skyscraper, I was at my seat in the office directly below what we'd be passing off as the surgery, watching as the broker met him at the door and guided him up to show off our grand illusion.

And I have to admit, it was good, right down to the sluggish performance Tenebrae offered when introduced to him as the body his brain would re-pattern. She seemed smaller. I don't know how she did it, but all of that natural grace I'd grown so used to over the last couple of weeks deserted her as she put on her act, coming over as timid and slightly lost in this expensive world she suddenly found herself in.

Fate bought it.

He had that smug look on his face and even cracked a lame joke about how, soon enough, he'd be inside her.

I expected her to break his neck. She was more than capable of snapping him like a twig. But instead, she just offered a girlish titter, playing the coquette.

He was more gullible than I'd expected.

They took him through to the surgery area, which looked more like a high-tech lab than a chop shop. Mel Kamahi had been busy in here, creating the visuals that would ultimately sell the illusion and talking our doctor through what the screens pretended. Fate listened to it all, nodding. Then they showed him the Crown of Thorns, which would dig just deep enough into his skull to hurt, and draw a trickle of blood in the process, whilst mapping his brain. There were two crowns, but no wires. Everything, our doc explained, was wireless, with the patterned data being stored as a huge single image on the immense servers that had been developed purely for the purpose of storing a human mind in all of its infinite computations and permutations.

Fate drank it all in.

The broker then put a case on the table between them. Inside was a data terminal, which, as he woke it, showed the details of the funds waiting to be transferred. "All it needs is the account for where the deposit is to be made, and it's all yours."

Thirty million is a lot of money, even on a computer screen where it's essentially abstract, just a string of numbers. Fate's face lit up. I could see the minute muscle spasms in his right hand as he wrestled with the idea of just reaching up and keying in the short sequence that would make him rich. We'd laid the foundation, this was the convincer. A very expensive convincer, but it needed to be.

I couldn't watch.

We'd done everything we could. It was down to Fate's inherent greed and vanity from here. How much did he want the money? How desperately did he need to believe he was the only man worth patterning our super soldiers on?

Enough was the answer.

He reached up to key in the account details.

"Excellent," the broker said, smoothly, triggering the transaction. "You are now a very wealthy man, Mister Fate."

Fate inhaled deeply, holding it, as though savoring the smell of the greenbacks that had just landed in his sweaty hands.

"So when do we do this?"

"As soon as possible," Imsen said.

Fate nodded. "Might as well get it over with. I'm here, the doc's here. Let's do this thing."

The broker looked at the doctor, pretending to seek permission and deliberately making it seem like Fate was asking a lot. The doc met his gaze. Looked around. Then called Tenebrae.

We'd got ourselves a con.

The doc told Fate to make himself comfortable as he put the crown of thorns on his head, then tightened the screws and continued to turn them until they'd broken through the skin and were biting into the bone. And then he turned them some more.

Fate cried out like a bitch.

I enjoyed that.

Fate being in pain was exactly what I wanted, and the more pain, the better.

Tenebrae reclined in the leather lounger beside him, her own crown resting lightly on her head. To sell the illusion we had to hurt her, too, but the doc would apply local anesthetic to numb the skin where the crown would pierce it.

Of course, nothing was going to happen. There was no miracle brain patterning software. Mel had created a video loop that would play on the big screen, making it look as though our tech was probing deeply into Fate's mind. The assassin was wearing a tiny earpiece that would allow me to feed her all the information she needed about Fate to sell the illusion that she knew him better than he knew himself.

Now, all we had to do was wait for the loop to play out.

After that, it was down to Mel to launch the hurrah and set the cat amongst the pigeons.

Fate was going to freak out.

Absolutely 100% guaranteed.

I must admit, being a conman was a step up from being a run of the mill Bleeder. I could get used to fucking with people's minds instead of just shooting at them.

I'm not sure what that said about me, if anything?

Tenebrae really sold it. She convulsed in the chair, her eyes rolling up into her skull to reveal the milky whites as she clutched at the leather lounger, bucking furiously. Sweat broke out on her brow, from beneath the thorns where the crown dug into her skin. Her mouth parted in a slight oh, breathless.

Behind her, the visuals Mel had put together continued to play, representing jags of data seemingly flowing from one mind into the other.

"I..." she said, the only word since she'd come in here. "Am not..." Fate stared at her. The doc stared at her. I stared at her. Captivated. "Me."

There was silence.

No one up there moved. Through the window I could see the dizzying neon lights of the cityscape that didn't reach all the way up to our make-believe clinic, it was like an ocean of color rippling away beneath us.

I didn't know what she was about to do.

We'd talked about how to sell the illusion, but in the end, it had to be something she was comfortable with. Something she could carry off for prolonged periods of time. She couldn't do the accent or the mannerisms, she hadn't been around him long enough to pick them up, so she needed to improvise. This was exactly what she was doing.

"It wasn't my fault," she said, turning to look at Fate in the chair beside her, his own pain forgotten about. The blood streamed down the side of his face. He looked like he wanted to bolt. But then, he thought he was looking at himself in a stranger's body. Who wouldn't want to run from that?

Tenebrae tore the crown from her skull, breaking more than just the supposed contact between their brains. Gasping for each breath, sweat glistening across her breastbone, she pushed herself out of the chair and crouched low. "It wasn't my fault. I didn't... It shouldn't have happened..."

Jesus fucking Christ, what was she doing?

I was up out of my seat ready to run up there and put a bullet in Fate's head on the spot. This was out of control. I shouldn't have tried to be clever. Keep it simple. I cursed.

On the screen, Tenebrae tore at her head—her hair had been shaved close to her scalp for the crown to nestle in place—as if trying to rip the demons out of it. It was a compelling image. She looked absolutely haunted. If I didn't know better, I'd have believed our psychic surgery had worked.

I looked at Fate.

It took me a second to see the track of tears on his cheeks. Because of the shadows, I'd thought it was blood, it wasn't.

He rubbed at his eyes.

I don't know how she'd done it, how she'd guessed, but she'd just taken one fuck of a gamble, and it looked as though it had paid off. Shadows moved across the screen. I tried to think. He obviously felt guilty about what had happened on some level, and she'd read it in him. How could I have missed it? Was I letting my own anger at what had happened cloud my judgment?

Could he be a victim in this, too?

I thought about it for a split second.

No.

There was no doubt in it, either. I was absolutely certain.

He was walking around, talking, breathing, taking money and acting the big man. He wasn't a victim. He certainly didn't think of himself as one. If he had, he'd have kept his head down. He wouldn't be taking these kinds of risks if he thought there was even the slightest chance that Swann and Martagan's killers would come back for him. So whatever guilt it was, it was post-traumatic, more like regret. Maybe his co-conspirators had promised him it wouldn't go down the way it had? That didn't change anything as far as I was concerned. What happened in that cemetery was absolutely his fault, no matter how he tried to wriggle out of responsibility.

"Has it worked?" Fate asked, crouching down over her, taking Tenebrae's head in his hands and tilting it so that she looked up at him, as though he hoped to see more of himself in her eyes than his glassy reflection. "I need to know... am I in there? Is that me? Is it?"

She looked up at him.

For a moment all I could think was that she was adoring him.

And then she spoke.

"I... I... feel... wrong." She told him, seeming to struggle as she looked for the words to explain what was going on inside her head. "It is loud... so... much... noise... So much going on. How do you live with it all? How do you cope?"

"Am I in there? Talk to me. Tell me something only I would know."

"I can feel you in here... like... like a parasite... I'm losing myself... aren't I?"

He didn't answer her.

Fate turned to the doc and the broker, looking for answers. "This isn't what you told me would happen. It was supposed to be a straight forward procedure. You'd simply overwrite her brain, re-pattern it so it was mine... but look at her. That's not what's happening. She's going out of her mind. You haven't overwritten her mind, you've just put another one in there with her," he said, sickened, "and it's slowly chewing through whatever is left of her... it's barbaric."

He was right, of course, if that was what was going on it would have been barbaric.

The doc looked at him. "That was always a risk," he said, not missing a beat. I needed to remember to pay him his bonus because she'd gone off script. "But the degradation should be a relatively swift process as your brain patterns consume hers. Humor me," the doc said, helping Tenebrae stand. "I'd be fascinated to see if her automotive skills have already been overwritten. Hit her."

I expected to Fate to refuse.

He didn't.

Without missing a beat he lashed out with his left hand, aiming a stinging slap at the side of the assassin's head. Tenebrae brought her right hand up to block it, catching his wrist and twisting hard to bring him down to his knees. Fate went down, but not because he was beaten. It was a ploy. He kept his weight on one supporting leg, then swept out the other, looking to cut her legs out from under her. She skipped the blow, bringing her leading foot down hard to stamp down on Fate's ankle. He punched upwards, driving his fist into her kidneys. Tenebrae rolled with the punch, again reacting with a staggering economy of movement, and had Fate's wrist in her grasp, arm extended, twisted to bare his elbow to her, and her knee resting against the joint so that the slightest increase in pressure would rip it apart.

"Excellent," the doc said, admiring his handiwork. "As I suspected, the subconscious, the muscle memory if you would, is the first to take root. She fights like a killer now."

"Yes, she does," Fate agreed, looking up at the black woman as she stared coldly back down at him. "I'd say that counts as a success, doctor."

"What do you remember?"

It was a good question. It was one I would have asked.

Fate waited for an answer.

When you lie your eyes betray you. They flicker up toward the left when you're lying—visually constructing an image. They flicker up to the right when you're accessing a memory. Everyone knows this. It's an easy tell. Of course, she wasn't making up anything, she was remembering the stories I'd told her over and over, so her eyes didn't betray her. I hoped it would be enough to reinforce the physical display she'd just put on. But a lot of it still hinged on Fate wanting to be fooled, meaning it came down to the same three things it had done from the start, greed, vanity, and gullibility.

He stared intently at her.

"Fragments," Tenebrae said.

"Describe one," he said.

So she did.

⌖

We were in Venice, city of trash.

Guerra, Swann and Martagan and me, walking side-by-side toward the main square. It's a protected place, so nothing's really changed despite the way the rest of the world has crowded in around it. The old Doge's Palace and all of those wonderful ruins tottering over the Grand Canal were just as they had been five hundred years before. Now though, it was a Warwulf-Blaze stronghold, and we'd just accepted a gig to protect a bunch of very rich commodity brokers who had just made a shitload of money on the backs of some dubious trades. One of them had been invited to test evolution against intelligent design, and drowned under the Rialto Bridge and left to feed the scavengers skimming the surface in the wake of the gondoliers.

That was when the others had called us in. Despite the riches, they were frightened little boys looking for someone to bleed for them.

They didn't fancy going out the same way. I tried to tell them I'd seen a lot worse, but they seemed intent on disbelieving me. Still, that helped me broker a good price. It was a win-win as far as I was concerned. It opened up a new client to us, for a start, which is always a good thing, and assuming we didn't screw the pooch and get ourselves killed, and obviously kept the clients alive, then who knew where it could lead?

Off this stinking trash heap, hopefully.

They used to think this place was romantic. I don't think they had any concept of what romance really was if they seriously thought that something reeking of piss, puke, and festering garbage was the stuff of love, then I admit, I know nothing of matters of the heart. To me, it would always be a city built on a mound of garbage. But, like a lot of romantic things, it was only surface deep, so I suppose there was that connection. Behind the façades of all of those perfect blue buildings and those chipped yellow walls the real heart of the city had been gutted and replaced with high tech office spaces connected to the world at large, money pulsing in and pulsing out of the hub that was Venice in a constant digital stream that was worth billions per second. We're talking mind-boggling amounts of money in trades, stuff the financial hubs couldn't begin to keep up with because the Venetian services were offering rates on the trades they couldn't match. The colonnades around St Mark's Square hid the building we needed to be in and presented all sorts of challenges in terms of putting up a proper defense, but there was no one else I'd rather at my side.

We were a team.

A pack.

The four of us.

They were expecting an attack. The intel was good. But then it ought to be, these guys were rich, rich people could pay for anything, including the betrayal of those who wanted them dead, it seemed. We put them in the safest place in the building, quite literally. In the vault. And time-locked it so even if we went down there was no way the hit squad was getting in there to kill our clients. We were their last line of defense—the four of us up against however many Bleeders the billionaires they'd screwed over had decided it was worth paying to make sure the job was done.

I tried to think of it as a holiday.

I mean, it's not often you get to kill people surrounded by so much history. Most of the world these days is all the same, basically. It is super towers, glass and neon, stuff that blurs into one as you move through it. There's so little with actual personality, so little that is unique. And even this wasn't really, it was just a front, everything behind it was absolutely 22nd Century.

Eight men went into the vaults. I could see Lisl Martagan's question, she didn't need to voice it. Eight men. Where were the women? Surely Warwulf-Blaze wasn't a male-only domain? There had to be women in the regional management structure, female brokers, too.

Were they being hung out to dry by the bastards who'd hired us? Left to fend for themselves?

It only took a few seconds to bring up the corporate directory and confirm that sixty percent of the employees in the Venice offices were female.

So much for equality.

"What do you want to do?" Martagan asked.

I wanted to do the job I'd been hired for. I didn't want to do anything pro-bono. That way lies madness. But I didn't want the blood of a bunch of innocent women on our hands if I could help it. "Go round up anyone you can find, give them a choice, evacuate or relocate down here where we can protect them. Those are the only two alternatives. Then get back down here and help Swann and Guerra get that gun emplacement secure. We don't know what to expect."

And that was the understatement of the year.

But it was my fault for misjudging our enemy and not taking into account the unique nature of our surroundings. A mistake I wouldn't make again. Venice is a city of islands, lots of little trash islands, joined by bridges. Implicit in that is the presence of water. I'd locked the people we were supposed to protect into a big steel vault that was basically separated from the murky depths by a few feet of brickwork foundation and not much else.

The explosions rocked the stanchions that supported the foundations. Rubble wept from the corners of the room, dry, dusty tears falling. If I'd known more about architecture, I'd have understood the significance of what I was seeing. But if wishes were fishes, I'd be a fucking shark.

A second wave of explosions followed fast on the aftershocks of the first. The building gave a deeper grumble. I looked around. "Where the hell are those bastards?"

"In a hurry to die?" Marco Guerra asked. He was always so bloody sarcastic. I think it came down to mummy issues. Maybe he hadn't had enough love when he was growing up.

"Always," I flashed him a grin. Let the fucker wonder what I was so happy about.

Not that I was happy for long.

Deep beneath us, I felt something tear. I heard it too, a second later, rising up through the old stones, then I heard the unmistakable drip drip drip of water splashing onto the marble floor.

"How far down are we?"

"How the fuck should I know?" Guerra said, helpfully.

The vault was locked. It wasn't like I could knock on the door and ask the guys inside. But a few seconds later as a piece of ancient plaster pushed in, collapsing under the pressure of the Grand Canal bearing down on it, I had all the answers I needed. We were under the canal. All it had taken were a few well-placed charges, controlled detonations, and the entire landscape of our fight changed as the water came pouring in and brought with it all the shit of the most romantic city in the world.

I heard screams up above.

Guerra and Swann had barely finished wrestling with the mobile gun turret, sinking its legs through the thin layer of marble over the wooden boards all the way down to the foundations of centuries-old garbage, as Martagan appeared with a handful of refugees and I realized the second flaw in my otherwise not-so-brilliant plan. I couldn't get them into the vault because we'd set the time lock. It was turning into an utter clusterfuck. "Get them somewhere safe," I yelled at Martagan, gesticulating wildly like I had an idea where safe was going to be down here. What I hadn't told anyone at this point was this was my first time at the rodeo. I'd never done this shit before. I could talk the talk, sure. I could make people think I was some great tactical visionary, and spin it every which way so they just assumed they'd somehow crossed my path a dozen times without realizing it, but the truth was I didn't have a clue. I was out of my depth. And everyone was about to find out just how far soon.

The third explosion was unlike anything I'd ever heard, and I realized then, a few seconds too late, what the hit squad intended.

They'd placed high-density explosives right beneath the vault, the first wave of explosives creating a tunnel in the trash island so they could swim in deeper to plant the second wave and finally blow their way right under the heavy vault.

Before the dust cleared on the third raft of explosions the gut-wrenching shriek of metal, stone and wood parting ways told us we were fucked. Well, not us, yet, but the eight men we'd ushered into that sealed cube who were now submerged in an airtight box running out of oxygen, with the sheer weight of canal water engulfing them enough to make sure they never managed to force that huge capstan door open again. We'd killed them by doing exactly what our enemy expected us to.

There was a lesson to be learned there.

Being predictable in this game kills.

I learned it. Too late for those eight money-grabbing bankers, but I learned it in time to save my own skin, which I figure is always the main thing with lessons.

The floor gave way beneath us, taking with it a small fortune in the form of the mobile gun turret we'd spent the best part of a morning installing. It hadn't fired a single shot in anger. It was the last time I was wasting my money on a big gun. From now on, assuming we got out of here alive, it was all about faith in my fellow man.

Time slows down when you're afraid. It does. Or at least the speed with which your brain processes things accelerates so greatly it seems that way. The hit squad rose up out of the ragged hole in the floor, their subaquatic gear dripping water, the dust of debris a cloud of camouflage around them.

I reacted first.

A single shot fired in panic, high and wide, but it started the killing.

There were four of them, four of us. Their suits were slick, oily, black, but had glo-lights on them that gave us something to aim at. Guerra was the first to make a kill. It was a lucky shot, whatever he says to the contrary. He'd been aiming for the center of mass, but the floor had shifted beneath his feet, throwing his aim off. The bullet, a hollow-point, took the man in the throat, opening up a huge sucking wound that sprayed arterial blood in an arc across the debris all around him. It was a spectacular first kill. Brutal. Bloody. There's nothing like arterial spray for the sheer mess of death it delivers. Guerra couldn't have made a cleaner kill if he'd tried.

But it didn't all go our way.

We nearly lost one of our own. As it was, the fall changed his life forever.

Swann.

I got him crippled that day.

I would give anything to be able to change what happened next, but I'm not a god, I can't simply rewrite life, scroll it back and play again because I don't like the way things turned out. Because of me, my best friend ended up in an exospine for the rest of his life.

It's the little things you don't think about. That vault took up maybe half of the surface area of the basement level, meaning they'd just blown out a huge portion of the building's foundations and absolutely undermined its integrity. There was no way it was going to hold against the forces at work on it. You take the skeleton out of a body, and the meat suit will collapse, same deal.

All sounds of very uncomfortable sounds echoed around us.

Then the bullets started to fly.

I dropped to one knee and loosed a volley, high, low, cutting across the line of sight in a harsh diagonal that chopped through another of their first wave. Oh yes, I wasn't stupid enough to think there were only four of them down there. Those first few were sent to smoke us out. The real force held back, waiting for the dust to settle. They knew what they were doing. They ought to, they were the ones who'd set the charges. They knew what the real damage would be, we were just improvising.

The brittle weeping of the walls only got worse as hollow points tore into them.

The increased weight on the shattered foundation struts meant it would only be a few more seconds until another part of the marble floor gave way. Again, the floor lurched beneath me, a precursor to the inevitable collapse as physics took it beyond the point of no return and everything buckled and collapsed inwards, sinking down into the water.

I was too busy worrying about what else was about to rise up out of that hole in the floor to realize the real risk was from the ceiling.

Lisl Martagan and I stood there side-by-side, guns locked and loaded, stupid grins on our faces, fighting for our lives and loving every minute of it because we'd just realized there was something broken in our psyche. We were *willing* more of the bastards to stick their heads up out of the water so we could shoot them. There's something almost sexual about killing with someone. It was better than any fuck we shared afterward, put it that way.

Only Guerra wasn't fighting.

He stripped off his guns and dove into the murky black under the building.

That was when I realized what was going on.

Swann was trapped beneath us. The sheer weight of the debris had dragged Swann underwater, and his injuries meant he couldn't free himself from the crushing press of the huge slabs of masonry that pinned his broken body to the trash island.

All Guerra had to go on were the slowly diminishing air bubbles. When that trail ran out, well, I don't need to tell you what that meant.

We stared at that hole in the floor, counting the bubbles as the gaps between them stretched out, willing the next heads to break the surface to be Guerra and Swann's.

They weren't. That was when the next wave of Bleeders surfaced, and the women behind us started screaming.

We went to work.

They rose up slowly, like the dead crawling out of the grave, first their faces, then their torsos and guns. Only, of course, it wasn't them, they were holographic projections. Our bullets tore clean through them and out the other side before we realized they didn't so much as flinch. That was when I realized they were coming up behind us. That's what the women had been screaming about—and why they weren't screaming now.

I spun around barely in time. The Bleeder was right behind me, arc-blade raised for a silent kill. I put a dozen hollow points in his chest, cutting him physically in half so as his knees buckled and his torso fell backward, he came apart.

I'd emptied my clip into him.

I didn't have time to reload. The bastards were on top of us.

And I was still grinning, realizing I was going to die laughing.

There are worse ways to go in this game.

But I didn't die. I dropped to one knee, scooping up the dead Bleeder's fallen blade and bringing it up in a savage arc, cutting the second Bleeder from balls to chin as he loomed over me.

Martagan dispatched her two with brutal precision, no wasted shells.

One died with a bullet to the eye, the other had his knees shot out from under him, and writhed around on the ground, telling us exactly who had sent them in before she killed him.

We went to them later and offered our services. After all, we'd killed two of their teams even if we'd lost our clients in the process. In operation terms, it was a failure, but technically it wasn't. None of our employers had taken a bullet. They'd slowly suffocated to death, trapped in that vault under water. No one had breached that vault. We'd kept them safe while they slowly ran out of oxygen. It was a technicality, but technicalities were important.

Guerra burst through the surface of the water, gasping and sucking in huge choking mouthfuls of air, Swann in his arms. He looked dead as Guerra laid him out on the floor and started the three short compresses of CPR on his chest, then break, then three, then break, until Swann regurgitated a dribble of water and gagged on the first breath of his new life as a cripple.

Sometimes I think he'd had rather died down there than spend the rest of his days dependent upon that exospine to move.

⌖

She told it perfectly.

She didn't embellish a single detail. No extemporization. It was exactly as I remembered it. It was exactly as Fate remembered, too. We were the only two people left in the world who had been through it, too, and understood the implications of how we wound up working for GenX and how that precious reputation we'd banked at never failing was built on the deaths of those eight money men who had died on a technicality.

He looked at her, sold.

She'd just described our first gig with the kind of detail only someone who'd lived through it could know, right down to the grief we felt at Swann's survival, which I know is an odd thing to say, but he was never the same after that. I think a part of him really did die down under that water.

It helped that I'd always known Lisl and him had a thing going on, especially on the back of a tough gig, the ones where we'd come closest to losing everything, and Tenebrae had dropped in that one line about the sex. It was that kind of veracity that sold it. As far as Fate was concerned the psychic surgery was a success. His brain was patterning itself on top of hers and bit by bit she was being given glimpses of the hell that was his life.

He'd seen her fight, now he'd heard her remember.

What she couldn't do was tell him what had happened under that water when I'd followed the bubbles down. That was something I'd have to live with. I made the choice. It was that or leave him to die. See, Fate doesn't know the half of it. I followed the air bubbles, though they slowed, the intervals between them becoming longer. It was hard to see. I was moving mostly by feel, reaching out in the darkness for the sharp edges of rubble, working my way along them, down until I saw the agitated mass in the water ahead and realized that Swann was trapped and thrashing around. I reached out for him, trying to work him free, but the more he thrashed about, the more absolutely trapped he became. I only had so much air in my lungs. I couldn't hold it forever. I could feel my chest tightening, burning, and really wanted to take a deep breath but I knew if I did my body would become complicit in my drowning, no matter what my mind wanted.

And he was fighting me hard. He wasn't dying easily. He was clinging desperately to life and would have killed me down there too if I hadn't acted. I swam up close to him, coming around behind him as he lashed out, and wrapped my arm around him to try and still the struggle but he was having none of it, so with my free hand I reached up and cupped my palm over his nose and mouth, and clung on grimly as the fight slowly left him.

The air bubbles no longer leaked between my fingers.

I had to move fast.

The problem was he was stuck. No amount of pulling would drag him free. And I was fast running out of lung capacity. So instead, I pushed, putting all my weight on the chunk of masonry that pinned him, and it moved. I knew what I had to do. I had to push that damn thing off of my friend and get him up to the surface, while every muscle in my body screamed out for oxygen.

I heard his spinal cord snap.

It was like no sound I'd ever heard in my life. It was absolutely sickening.

And Tenebrae had been right when she said it would have been better if he'd died down there—or stayed dead. But that was my burden to carry. No one else knew about it. I was never going to tell anyone. Confession isn't good for the soul. Confession gives your enemies ammunition to use against you. I paralyzed Swann, then brought him back from the dead and made him live as a cripple. It wasn't the explosions, it wasn't the collapse, it was me. Our first mission together. But, what happened under the water stayed under the water. I could live with the secret. It wasn't tearing me apart or giving me sleepless nights. As far as I was concerned, better an exospine than a box in the ground. Now, of course, Swann would be able to tell me if I was right. He'd need a Ouija board to do it, mind you, but if anyone could get a message through from the other side, it was him.

While the assassin was playing her part, Mel Kamahi had her own job to do, and it was every bit as important. The hurrah was when we took everything Fate thought he knew and turned it upside down. It was when vanity was transformed into paranoia.

There's some stuff I should explain, how the world works out there. There is no church, not anymore, but there is a new god: the machine. You get some hackers who have these chairs, rigs they call them, that are biomech stuff, a bridge between the hacker and his wonderland. I've seen a few, they are more like the pod of an octopus's mantle, with these great organic vines and suckers that fasten onto the rig's occupant, burrowing down into their reptilian hindbrain where thought and action co-exist. It's one frightening fucking thing to look at, to be honest, but it has to be worse to sit in it.

Mel's rig was a little less nightmarish to look at, but who knew what went on when she jacked in?

Not me, and I didn't want to. My only demand was that I didn't want her taking any unnecessary risks. She was committed to the cause, but I'll be honest, I think there's a kind of addiction that goes on with flatlining. It's not normal. It's like those guys who go in for auto-erotic asphyxiation because it's supposed to be the ultimate high when you jerk off and blow your brain by flirting with death at the same time. Dumb in other words. The kind of shaming death when it goes wrong that corps have used forever to undermine the credibility of the guy they just took out. But like I said, if the machine is their new god, then jacking into it so completely, separating your mind or soul or whatever it is that's essentially you from the flesh to exist purely inside the machine must be akin to a religious experience. Think about it, a Flatliner died and become one with the machines they mastered, just for a while, a couple of minutes, never longer than that, and then they came back. No interfaces, no bridges or joins between them, they were a spirit inside the machine, alive as a thought process, digital impulses, nothing else.

Do that enough, and you're going to get hooked.

Nothing is going to be enough after that.

No matter how on fire they are, there's just no way they can physically hit keys and trigger commands at the speed of thought—faster—it just can't be done. There's always a layer of impulse and reaction to it. And for a certain kind of person, someone who lives and dies traffic and signals and interfaces, nothing less than that is ever going to be satisfying again once they've tasted it. It's like the forbidden fruit, I guess. Bite into that apple, and every other apple's just going to taste sour in comparison.

There's an entirely new breed of short-lived Flatliners out there, earning top dollar for the risks they're taking, knowing that one of these days the shock paddles won't bring them back.

I understood the addiction, but that didn't mean I had to like it.

I didn't want to be like Fate.

But, and I hate to admit it, I was happy to use her addiction to get what I wanted in this case.

Everything had to be timed just right. It's difficult to orchestrate a good con, especially when you need the mark to work things out for himself in a certain order, so you are drip feeding them revelations, steering them toward the reactions you want. When you're a Bleeder, the job's pretty straight forward. You go into a place knowing that you're going to have to be prepared to lay your life down to make sure the other guys don't walk away with whatever it is you're protecting. I was beginning to grasp exactly what being Randall Fate must have been like, all those strings to pull. It wasn't just about getting the best price, it was about thinking ten steps ahead of the enemy, anticipating everything they might do to us and making sure we had a contingency in place to counter it.

I could pretend to understand what, exactly, Mel was doing,

but in reality, all I saw were a few fluttering eyelashes and then nothing, she just lay there in that rig, lifeless, the low tone of the heart monitor offering the single longest note known to man. I had the shock paddles in my hands and a clock ticking down over my head. I had no idea if she was in, what kind of defenses she was having to battle her way through, though I envisioned them as something like an arcade game throwing barriers up against her that she needed to defeat to pass on to the next level. What can I say? I like simple. A nice graphical representation of the spider's web that is the net, with cyber dogs to hunt the hacker down and chow down on their brains if they're caught. I do know that there used to be communities in there, bulletin boards and message boards, gathering places, but that was before the corporations got a grip on things, now there are just ghost towns no longer curated by a soul. Abandoned. There are relics, of course, but no one would dare go there for long for fear of what traps the corps might have laid. You don't want to be seen to think too loudly or differently these days. You don't want to stick your head up above the parapet if you value your freedom.

Though what sort of freedom is it when the corporations own you, body and soul?

I counted down the seconds.

Two minutes was the deal.

Anything longer than that was asking for trouble. Every extra second increased the possibility of her not coming back. But it also meant she had longer to do what she needed to do. I watched the second-hand tick remorselessly on, counting out the first minute. The dull, flat note of the monitor was enough to drive me out of my mind. It just went on and on and on, never seeming to end. My hands were shaking. I was sweating. I wished she'd been able to just go in normally, but the defenses on these corporation systems nowadays were so intricately layered it would take a team of hackers executing perfectly synchronized attacks to breach their system. This way she could issue an infinite number of coordinated commands all by herself, lightning fast. She'd convinced me it was the only way into GenX.

I believed her.

Ninety seconds.

I wish I knew what was going on in there.

One hundred.

Twenty more and I had to pull her out, no matter what.

Fifteen.

But I wasn't charging up the paddles. I hadn't slathered the conductive gel over the shock pads.

Ten.

Was I really prepared to leave her in there longer than two minutes?

Two minutes is the magic number: when there's no blood being pumped into the brain, the nerve cells in the cerebral cortex begin to die after that. The nerve cells in the midbrain that control unconscious activity such as breathing can last thirty minutes, though. Thirty minutes. What could she do in there in thirty minutes? If I knew for sure she'd be able to function pulling her out of there would be even more difficult than it already was, but without the oxygen and glucose of fresh blood pumping through the system the oxygen in the stagnant blood would be used up by the cerebral cortex in two minutes. That magic number.

Anything beyond that, and even if I brought her back there was the risk of brain damage.

I watched the clock.

Five seconds.

And I still wasn't reaching for the gel. Even if I did right now, right this second, the paddles wouldn't be charged in time.

So how long was I prepared to go to get what I wanted?

Three minutes. One hundred and eighty seconds. Almost half as long again as was safe. I'd willingly starved Mel Kamahi's brain of oxygen, knowing exactly how much damage I was doing to her because I needed to know she'd succeeded.

That was how badly I wanted Fate.

I put the charged paddles against her breast and shocked her.

The hacker's body convulsed, back arcing. Spittle flew from her mouth where she reflexively bit down on her tongue. There was no blood because her heart wasn't pumping. I shocked her again. There was no change in that damned note. She wasn't coming back. I yelled at her, willing her to hear my voice wherever she was and focus on it. I cranked the charge up, knowing the jolt would burn her. I didn't care. She was coming back. She was.

I shocked her again.

The shiver ran from her into me.

The note didn't change.

Again.

I cranked the charge up as high as it would go.

She was dead. We were moving into four minutes, and she wasn't coming back. I didn't know what to do. But I couldn't give up. Another shock.

Her breasts came up to meet the paddles, then her back slammed back down into the rig. Two things happened at once, the note broke, the sound fractured by silence, and her eyes opened.

She stared at me.

She couldn't speak. She was choking on that breath that had been almost four minutes in coming.

I wasn't about to tell her how long she'd been out.

"Is it done?"

She nodded.

"You... left me... in there..." she accused.

I shook my head. I couldn't look her in the eye. Instead, I looked down at the paddles in my hands. "I couldn't get you out. You weren't coming back."

"Liar," she said.

⌖

Now, all we could do was wait.

I'm not the most patient guy at the best of times, but I was itching for something to happen.

I was half tempted to take a job, just to keep my mind occupied.

There's nothing like shooting something to stop you from being bored.

But I couldn't concentrate, not properly, and the last thing I wanted to do was get myself perforated by some stray hollow point before I'd finished playing with Fate.

So I did the only thing I could do.

I waited.

Thankfully not in some flea pit motel now, but in a rather comfortable suite rented out by the broker, Imsen, through a shadow company that traced back to our old friends at Warwulf-Blaze. Close to the action, but not too close. The view was incredible, looking out over the amazing crush of humanity, all of the bright lights of the big city blurring through the streaks of rain—climate controlled, not natural. It never rained here naturally, but the men with the money made it happen, just like they made everything else happen. Each one of those raindrops had probably cost someone somewhere a small fortune. I would have laughed if it wasn't quite so tragic. Rain farms. Who'd have thought we'd ever get quite so environmentally fucked up?

"Why isn't he freaking out?" I asked, without turning around.

The others were behind me, playing a hand of cards in a scene that mirrored my memories of Wan Chai plaza what seemed like another life ago. The waiting never changes. Neither does how people do it.

"He will," Mel assured me. "It's all in there, everything he needs to know to realize the sky is falling."

"I know, I know," I said. "But can't we just give it a helping hand?"

"Maybe," Tenebrae said, taking me by surprise. "Hire him to steal the information, or at least something related to it, something that names him as patient zero."

In other words, hand it to him on a plate.

It was a risk.

But I really hated waiting.

"No," I said, an idea already beginning to take shape. It was outrageous enough that it just might work. "We turn it around. We hire him to protect the information, not steal it."

"Who from?"

"Me," I said, smiling. I knew the one thing that was guaranteed to make him take the job—the chance to go head-to-head with Marco Guerra one last time.

"That'd put the cat amongst the pigeons," Gant agreed. He had that look on his face. The one that said he was itching to get into trouble. I knew exactly how he felt.

"He'll bite. He'll want to know what it is I'm so desperate to get my hands on, which means he'll take the job just so he can get his hands on it first, then he'll find what Mel planted and slowly but surely the implications will settle in. Then all the money in the world won't feel like enough to that greedy bastard." I turned to the broker, Imsen. "He can't know it comes from us, obviously, so you'll need to use a third party to broker the deal, and make it irresistible."

"You're not really planning on going up against him, are you?" Rowell Gant asked.

"What do you think?"

Gant looked at me. I looked at him. We weren't exactly having a 'moment.' He grinned. "I think you're just about mad enough to."

He was beginning to know me. I half-nodded. It wasn't a shrug. It wasn't a no or a yes.

"It needs to be convincing," I told the broker.

He nodded. "Leave it to me."

Things were getting interesting.

Fate had a new team. He'd put the word out a few hours after the broker's man had made contact. Despite a couple of catastrophic failures, Bleeders were lining up to die for him. I'll never understand that kind of desperation. He had his team picked before nightfall.

I wanted him to see me coming.

That was important to me.

So, the first thing I did was make sure we got in there first, infiltrating the site—which we'd scoped out to make sure was suitable, not too high profile a location, not too remote or well-defended— we'd be hiring him to protect, and planting a series of squibs and other devices to make it appear that the place was coming under attack when it wasn't. Smoke and mirrors. I wasn't about to risk my own skin if I didn't have to, but I wanted him to think I'd come out from under my rock and really sell the idea that this information hidden away on their servers was that important to me. He was like a child. If I wanted it, he'd want it. Simple as that.

Swann had been an idiot savant when it came to blowing shit up; the guy just had the touch. He could plant a charge and trigger a chain reaction that would have toppled bricks and mortar all the way to heaven's gate if he set his mind to it. Gant wasn't Swann. They didn't have the same warped mindset. But they did share a love of blowing things up which meant he was the man for the job.

I think it's a male thing.

We went in together dressed in the bland coveralls of workmen. No one ever looks twice at the grunt labor they think of as beneath them. It means you can hide in plain sight. Mel Kamahi made sure we had all the paperwork and work orders we needed to make it look as though we were meant to be there. It's amazing what lies you can tell with a computer terminal. No one questioned us as we went about the business of rigging the tower up, including secreting audio speakers in the vicinity to relay what would sound like all hell breaking loose when we wanted it to. Mel jacked into the security system, piggybacking their video feed so we could stream surveillance footage directly to our own monitors and watch Fate, which, I'll admit, gave us an unfair advantage, but who said we had to play fair?

With eyes and ears on the place, and the pyrotechnics show rigged, Imsen's man closed the deal, offering a contract that wasn't too good to be true, but was far from insulting. He sold it with the one hook I knew Fate wouldn't be able to resist: "Marco Guerra's got a crew together, and they're after stuff we've got buried deep on the n-server. Under no circumstances is he to be allowed to get his hands on it, bring the place down around his ears if you have to, but do not let him walk out of there with that information. Do we understand each other?"

I smiled as the two shook on it and Fate's downfall was sealed.

We took up positions and waited.

It didn't take long. We'd dangled just enough intel to ensure Fate didn't hang about.

I watched Fate's boys roll in, and gave my old mentor time to batten down the hatches. He looked ten years older than he had when we'd gone into GenX. Time wasn't being kind to him. I hoped that meant the bastard wasn't sleeping. Yes, I'm that petty. I wanted to get inside his head and crawl about in the filth of his mind for a bit, making enough mess to be sure he'd never sleep again. That, in my book, would be a win.

The crew he'd brought with him looked wet behind the ears. I couldn't understand why he'd turned us over for them, but of course, he hadn't. This motley crew was the best he could get at short notice. There was no loyalty or experience there, which helped. They'd spook. And spooked, they'd abandon Fate.

I gave him time to make his preparations. I knew his routines. He was a creature of habit. Then I had a young guttersnipe I paid a few bucks move in to set up the remote-triggered hologram, knowing he'd have his eyes focused on the outside, looking for my approach.

I waited.

I wanted him antsy.

Itchy.

A couple of minutes later, there I was, large as life, on all of the monitors he'd got focussed on the plaza outside, far enough away he wouldn't see through the illusion too quickly. I'd made sure he knew that was where the threat came from—mirroring our last job. There was sewer access to the left of the plaza, through a drainage network. We'd set up barriers and a tent in broad daylight. The holographic specter hinted that my team had gone in that way. There was a nice symmetry to it even if I'd got no intention of going inside. I just wanted to keep him in there long enough for curiosity to finally get the better of him. We'd put on a show, of course, but it was all about time. Eventually, locked in there long enough, Fate would start digging.

Mel Kamahi had hidden it well enough, but not too well, all it needed was for him to find the first dossier sanctioning the payments for Sleeper Zero—his file—and it would all start to unravel. A couple of layers down he'd find the termination order. When the corporations wanted you dead, you were dead. No amount of money could save you. And that was the hurrah. Think about it, why would they need the unpredictable, uncontrollable original out there destabilizing their investment when they had everything they needed to make the perfect fighting machine a thousand times over? Ten thousand. An army of Fate's.

As of now, he was replaceable.

That was the truth he hadn't thought of. He'd made himself obsolete. That was the spanner in the works moment when he realized they'd got his brain patterns in storage and he'd seen with his own two eyes just how easily they could re-pattern anyone to give them his unique skillset.

Why would the corporation want to keep him alive?

Then it was just a short hop skip and a jump to realizing just how much trouble he was in, us to the left, the corporations to the right, nowhere to run except back to the Gene Sculpt Clinic in Dubai where he thought his brain images were in storage, playing right into my hands.

God, I'm good.

I am.

All humility aside, he was dancing to my tune.

I wanted him frightened.

Frightened men make mistakes.

I wanted to enjoy this.

It was a once in a lifetime chance to savor revenge.

Fate was a dead man walking.

He just didn't know it yet.

But he would, any second now.

I am a very bad man.

I am.

"Time to have some fun," I said, and triggered the first explosion.

The shockwaves rocked the building.

We could see the way the walls bowed outwards, barely contained by the tolerances of glass, iron, and steel, stretched to the limits all carefully calculated to add to the illusion of an attack, and watched intently as Fate's team took up defensive stations as they waited for the smoke to clear. They couldn't see us because we weren't there, but they didn't know that. I triggered the first audio, which sounded like a barrage of gunfire and ran a brief sequence that let off some of the squibs. If it looks like a fish and sounds like a fish, it's a fish. This looked like an attack, sounded like an attack, so to the guys in there this was an attack.

Another controlled detonation shook the foundations.

The explosions were important. We hadn't had time to rig hydraulics to fake the aftershocks, so we needed the next best thing, real honest to god damage. The majority of tricks we'd employ in the fake attack were digital though, and far less spectacular. They would, of course, look very, very real on Fate's screens, which was the important thing. Mel had created a layer of damage simulations she'd lay across the feeds from Fate's cameras to make it look as though the corridors leading up to their redoubt were in ruin, lots of smoke, debris, twisted metal, a few screaming people. I'd seen it before. He'd buy it. She was that good. Half the time, I think she could have actually pulled the whole con off without us, and just liked to let me feel useful.

I watched Fate on a dozen screens.

That meant I had twelve different views of that glorious moment when he first saw my hologram out in the plaza.

They're right, you really do turn white when you see a ghost.

He stared, and he stared.

Then, as far as he was concerned, my ghost stepped back into the shadows. The guttersnipe had killed the hologram.

He knew I was coming for him.

I'd emerge later, inside, from a different projector, cementing the illusion. I wanted Fate to feel the noose tightening around his neck. It needed to feel remorseless. No matter how he countered, no matter what tricks he tried, I wanted him to know that nothing he did was working. And I knew how he would respond to most eventualities—we'd fought side-by-side through fifty conflicts. You learned a lot about a man in that time.

I'd planted several remote-triggered holographic projectors inside the compound.

He could blow three of them sky high, the fourth would still come online no matter how much damage was done, how many hollow points ripped into the walls, how many detonations went off or supporting walls came down, the sheer relentless progress of my ghost would appear inevitable. One by one those holographic projections would come online always a little closer to where Fate was dug in until there was nowhere left to run.

Then Fate would use whatever he could get his hands on to bargain for his life.

Which was exactly what I wanted.

It worked like a charm.

The final hologram flickered into life no more than thirty feet from his door.

I spoke to Fate through his wireless comms link. I could have used the hidden speakers, but the idea of being right there inside his head just appealed too much.

I could see him trying to work out what trickery I was employing, how we'd hijacked his radio, and come to the realization that he was working on the same frequency we'd always operated on. Old habits die hard. Bleeders die harder. The projection was far enough away—and thus small enough on the screen—that he couldn't see that its lips weren't moving as I said, "I only want the files, Fate. That's it. I couldn't give a shit about you. What happened between us, that's the past. I'm a big boy, I'll get over it. But you need to know I don't particularly want to kill you, you have options. You don't have to die here. Just give me what I want, and I'll forget you ever existed."

That was so close to the truth it hurt.

"You never were that forgiving in life, Marco," Fate said, grimly. "Why should I think you'll be that forgiving in death?" He seemed to be looking directly at me. It was unnerving. His gaze stripped away the levels of anonymity and distance between us. Mel had rigged the webcam in his screen to relay its video feed back to us. He didn't even know it was on, never mind broadcasting. It was an old hack. Anything more sophisticated, I'm almost sure he'd have spotted. Sometimes the old ways are the best. He stared at the grainy image of my hologram out in the corridor beyond the room he was holed up in, waiting for me to answer him.

"I'm a new man," I said.

"Suppose I believe you," Fate said, tentatively. "What's so important about this information? What is it I'm letting you get your hands on? Are we talking nuclear winter level shit here, or just menopausal-bitch-intent-on-making-things-bad-for-you kind of thing?"

"It's private," I said. It was.

"Oh come, come, you don't expect me to put out and not get something in return?"

"I'm not in the mood to bargain or make deals."

"Pity," Fate said. "It'd be like old times, you whining, me making you my bitch."

I let him have his moment.

Well, I gave him maybe ten seconds to enjoy it then dropped the hammer. I killed the remote hologram, counted to ten, and triggered the last one, which came to life in the corner of the room, just on the periphery of Fate's vision. He turned his head, doing an almost comic double take, then just muttered, "Oh, you clever, clever fucker, Marco." He didn't waste any ammo. He saw through the illusion. He was meant to. The whole point was that I wanted him to know I'd been in there already, that I'd breached their security, and that I could have had whatever it was I wanted and disappeared without ever facing off with him.

I hadn't intended on activating this last hologram. I don't know why I did. Fate, I guess. Just seeing him in there riled me. Stripped me of my calm, calculating edge. If it had been Gant or Tenebrae that had pulled a stunt like this right at the end, I'd have gone off my fucking nut and torn a strip off them, left Gant hobbling around gelded, and I don't even want to admit where my mind just went to with her. It was a dark, dark place. I'd blown my load.

"Surprise," I said, wishing I'd shown a little more restraint instead of being hungry to show Fate who was in charge. It's arrogance. I know it is. What's the point of being the cleverest person in the room if no one else knows you are?

"What's your game?"

I thought about saying nothing, but I'd already played my cards. He wasn't going to go rooting through the n-server if he thought I'd already been in there and got whatever it was I was after. I needed to think on my feet, find some way to recover the situation.

I hate doing stupid things.

I tried to think, but only ended up speaking before I'd thought it through. "What if I told you two days ago I'd stood exactly where you are right this second, hands braced on the same dumb terminal, and rigged a bomb that is counting down as we speak, ticking out the last seconds of your life?"

"I'd say well played," Fate said. "But I don't think you'd do that. Not your style. Women poison, fanatics bomb, I think you'd want to be up close when you stuck the knife in, nice and personal, looking me in the eye and coming out with some pithy line because that's the kind of bastard you have always been."

"People change."

"Are you talking about you or me?"

"Maybe both of us."

"Serious question," Fate said, looking straight at me through the monitor. "What's your win here, Marco? What will make you happy? What result has both of us walking away from this mess in one piece to play again another day?"

It was the million dollar question. What would make me happy? It wasn't just about killing Fate. If it had been, I'd have done that days ago.

"I want to break you," I said. It was the first truthful thing I'd said to him in a long time. "I don't mean kill you. I've got absolutely no interest in you being dead, or in you bleeding, Randall. I want to break you. I want to leave you so emotionally shattered you curl up in a corner, just rocking back and forth in your own shit wishing it was all over."

"Well, I'll be honest," Fate said. "I'm not sure I can work with that. What's in it for me?"

"Nothing. But you asked what would make me happy."

"Good point. Okay, let's revise that, what's the least you'd consider a win? Maybe we can meet somewhere in the middle, beat the Corps for once?"

"I want what's on the n-server," I said.

"I don't believe you, Marco. You never were a very good liar," oh if only you knew, my friend, if only you knew. "I don't think there's anything on there—or if there is, you've already been in and got it. Despite what you said, this is all about us. You and me."

I smiled a 'fuck you' smile.

"Look for yourself." It took a moment for what I was saying to sink in, like a dare. "If you doubt me, look for yourself. You're in there. The system is wide open to you. Look. And then when you know what it is they've got you defending, maybe you'll change your mind?"

Do it, I urged silently. It was a bloody good job he couldn't see my face.

"Is this your great plan? You want me to fuck around inside my employer's system, get caught, and end up in corporate jail? It's not exactly audacious, Marco."

"Just do it," I said. "I won't tell if you don't. Or are you frightened you can't pull it off with me watching? Never had you pegged for performance anxiety?"

His fingers moved involuntarily, and I realized he was triggering a command to take the terminal down into root mode and start digging around in the n-server. Without knowing what he was looking for it could take a while, even if Mel had planted a few nice juicy bread-crumbs for him to follow.

"What am I looking for?" He asked.

"You'll know it when you see it," I said. I wasn't giving him any more than that.

"Why should I trust you?"

"You shouldn't."

"Never a truer word, eh?" Fate said.

Beside him the other Bleeders he'd brought in were milling around aimless and obviously more than a little anxious, not enjoying our reunion. They didn't know how to react. It was throwing them off their game. They expected to fight. They were prepared for it. When you go into a combat situation a lot of the time, you are psyching yourself up, getting the blood and adrenalin pumping. When you stand around doing nothing, not even waiting—where at least you are tense, on edge—then you climb down. It's just natural. You can't be on indefinitely. It just doesn't work that way. We were denying them the chance to do what they were good at: bleeding.

This whole barter-taunt thing we'd got going on was out of their comfort zone.

A lot of what happened next would be down to their inexperience.

The shooting *would* start soon enough. Fate and I both knew that. The standoff was purely temporary. The one thing Fate hadn't realized was that I'd already decided exactly how it would begin, not just when and where.

"You can turn that stupid thing off, you know?" Fate said, meaning the hologram.

"I can," I agreed. "But I rather like how uncomfortable it is making you."

"Of course you do."

I couldn't see what was happening on the screen, so had no real way of knowing how close Fate was to the Sleeper Zero file. The only thing I knew for sure was that he hadn't found it yet.

That changed a minute later.

It was the rhythm of his typing that gave it away—it quickened and became just that little bit more erratic than it had been a few seconds earlier, and then stopped dead.

I waited, watching his face, waiting for the truth about Sleeper Zero to sink in.

There was no mistaking it then.

I resisted the temptation to think my job here was done. It wasn't. Things were just starting to get interesting.

These are the little victories you have to savor.

Another string of commands, another twist of the face. Mel's gingerbread trail was tantalizing. Deliberately so. I knew there was an image of the meat factory we'd stumbled into on our penultimate gig, that was the hook along with the promise of Sleeper Zero's identity. He didn't look at me. He kept executing commands, ignoring everything around him. Finally, he looked up and said simply, "Was this your doing, Marco?"

He could have meant it two ways: one did I plant the material, or two did I engineer the whole thing that would end ultimately in his replacement and death. It was a good thing he couldn't see my face.

"It's too big a coincidence," he continued. "You're after some buried files in the n-server, and I just happen to be the subject of them. You really must try harder next time," Fate mocked.

"I have no idea what you are talking about," I lied. "You're not the subject of anything. I was paid to retrieve information that proves collusion between two of the major corps, GenX and Warwulf-Blaze, we are talking massive manipulation, including the deliberate production of genetically enhanced foodstuff containing rapid carcinogens in an attempt to regulate population control. They are deliberately killing non-profitable people, Randall. I couldn't give a fuck about you. This is bigger than you." And if it had been true, it would have been. The important thing was Mel Kamahi had buried the right 'proofs' for that story right alongside the whole Sleeper Zero reveal.

I knew he'd found them when Fate muttered a guttural, "Fuck."

I didn't push it. I waited for him to make the first move.

"Marco?"

"What?"

"We need to call a truce. Like you said, this thing is bigger than me, bigger than you. I can help you. I'm on the inside. I can get this stuff out for you and make it look like I did my job here at the same time. We can both be winners here." And there was the Randall Fate I knew and loved, always looking for the angle.

"And I should just trust you? After what happened?"

"I'm trusting you, dude," he said, bluntly. "Pick a rendezvous, pick the meet time, control everything. I'll turn up, and we can trade off the intel. You get exactly what you need, I get to pay you back for before, and we draw a line under it. Shit... I might even need to hire you myself, bro, the way things are going. You're the best Bleeder out there. What do you say?"

"We'd need to sell it," I said. "They've got cameras everywhere, all angles covered. We'd need to make it believable. I can't just turn my crew around and walk away. No one is gullible enough to buy that."

"So that's exactly what we do," Fate said. "We put on a fireworks display."

"Even so... I don't know," I said, trying not to sound too eager to bite his hand off.

"I know you've got eyes in here, watch me," Fate said, and I saw him draw a small thumb-drive from one of the pockets of his suit and slip it into the interface. "I'm downloading everything you need right now. You can watch me carry it out of here. I can't do more than that."

He was downloading more than that, of course. He was pulling everything he could find about Sleeper Zero from the n-server, too and using the pretense of downloading my files as cover.

I'm glad that my old mentor is as predictably clever and devious as ever.

He pocketed the drive. "I've got it. Everything. Now let's make this exciting for the folks at home, shall we?"

"One thing," I said.

"Name it," Fate said, a little too readily. He still had that habit of letting his mouth make promises his ass couldn't keep.

"Someone has to die. There's no way your paymasters would believe we walked away without casualties."

"Yours or mine?"

"I'm not picky, both, someone has to die to sell it," I said. None of his crew could hear the communication, Mel had made sure of that. I don't know how she'd done it, jamming frequencies or something, but it meant that it was just me and him, and I wanted to know if he'd sell his team out again for his own survival, or if what had happened with us had really changed him like he claimed.

"Okay, I'll make sure it happens. You just concentrate on making the show look convincing."

In one line he'd proved beyond a shadow of a doubt he was as big a bastard as always. Okay, I'll admit it, I'm glad this particular leopard hadn't changed his spots.

"In the spirit of our newfound cooperation," I said. "I should tell you I wasn't kidding before. There's a nice little package in that room counting down. I reckon you've got about thirty seconds 'til it blows. You might want to take cover behind that bank of steel benches behind you."

He didn't say a word.

Fate dove for cover, hurling himself to the ground a split second before the C4 blew.

It was a contained blast, more flash than bang, even so, it brought a huge chunk of the roof down around them, and with an ungodly roar kicked up enough dust and debris to cover what I was up to for a couple of seconds, as a second charge took the door off its hinges and left the place wide open to attack. I hate explosions. They're the epitome of destruction, absolutely out of control even when supposedly channeled. It's like saying scorched earth is showing restraint. Some things, by their very nature, are just out of control.

I nodded to Mel, who triggered the squibs and a second later, amid the chaos, the sound of machine-gun fire ripped through the confines of the passage. If Fate had been paying attention, he would have realized there was no accompanying puff of masonry dust as the bullets tore into the wall behind him, because there were no bullets.

Fate kept his head down.

The rest of his crew were dazed and confused, stumbling about in the smoke.

Fate hadn't warned them, so they'd been caught in the explosion.

He really was a piece of work.

I didn't know their names.

One of them, the muscle, was bleeding from a head wound. The blood mingled with the dirt on his face. He staggered, needing the twisted metal frame of the bench for support. The detonation had been loud. Deliberately so. Noise fucks with the balance. Your ears are precariously tuned instruments. He'd be reeling for a couple of minutes, trying to get his bearings. The landscape could change a lot in that time.

I watched intently, waiting to see how long it would take for Fate to throw his newest disciple under the bus.

It happened quicker than I could have hoped. As his man stumbled around, Fate put a single bullet in the back of his head, and he went down. To anyone watching playback, it would look like one of our barrages had taken him out, only, of course, we hadn't fired a single shot.

Fate started screaming, "Man down!" and his cohorts came out shooting blindly.

It was absolute and beautiful chaos.

It couldn't last, of course.

We'd only laid enough charges to play out the charade for a few minutes, but that was a lifetime when you were under fire.

Beside me, Gant was itching to get down there and really get his hands dirty.

"I don't understand why you won't just let me go down there and kill the miserable fucker, seriously, all this smoke and mirrors shit gets really old, really fast."

"Because," I said slowly. "I've got no intention of killing him. That's far too easy, and nowhere near satisfying enough. I want the bastard to live forever. Trust me, I think you'll approve. You're just about twisted enough to truly appreciate it."

He didn't look convinced, but he didn't argue either way.

We followed Fate's escape on the monitors, enjoying the show as he hammed it up for the audience. Had we actually been working together to rob GenX it would have been nothing short of genius. As it was, there was a beauty to the dance, like old lovers so intimately familiar with each other's bodies, we knew just how to manipulate each other for the most pleasure.

The only thing that was missing from our side of the equation was a casualty.

But when it came right down to it, I just wasn't like Fate. I couldn't sacrifice Gant to sell the illusion. One corpse would have to be enough.

I saved a couple of tricks until Fate was almost out, but the best was absolutely saved for last.

Tenebrae.

The assassin faced him across the plaza.

She was dressed in full combat gear, ready to give the old man the fight of his life.

He came out of the place at a full run and skidded to a halt, facing her. He recognized the assassin immediately. I could see the cogs whirring away inside his head. She was him. She thought like him. She fought like him. She knew all his moves and shared all of the instincts he had as a base. And here she was, on-site with the corporation that wanted to use his brain patterns to build a super army of Bleeders they owned and controlled. Meaning he didn't know if he was about to go toe-to-toe with his own worst nightmare or if she was some kind of temptation being dangled in front of him. I could see him thinking: what will happen if I kill her? Does it end here? Can I still get out of this or is it too late?

She walked slowly toward him, facing down the three of them as they emerged with all the bravura of a gunslinger.

He stopped.

Waited.

"What are you doing here?"

"I have my orders," she said, four wonderfully creepy words. He didn't wait for her to expand on them. He pushed one of his crew away, shoving them hard to the right, and made a break for it. Head down, arms and legs pumping furiously, he ran for his life, the assassin on his heels. She moved lightly, her body a thing of beauty as she moved, tight, taut, toned, and utterly relentless. She covered the ground between them in seconds. It didn't matter how fast Fate ran, she was faster.

She had an arc-blade in her fist, glittering against the rising sun.

For a moment I thought she was actually going to cut him down. That wasn't part of the plan. She was just meant to drive home the fear, reinforcing the fact that now that his brain had been patterned there was nowhere left he could run, someone would always find him because they shared all of those formative memories. The corporation knew him better than he knew himself.

Fate wasn't helpless though; far from it.

He had a contingency.

He always had a contingency.

It was the way he worked.

In this case, it came in the form of a fifth team member, a getaway driver.

I was impressed. He was thinking outside of the box. In all the time I'd run with him we'd never employed a fifth crew member, even one that stayed on the outside. The car surged onto the plaza itself, nearly mowing down a gaggle of youths that were lost in whatever teenage world preoccupied them these days. There were yells and screams followed by bravado-fueled curses as the passenger door of the black car flew open. The getaway driver yanked hard on the wheel. The car slewed sideways across Fate's path. Tenebrae was still twenty meters away. Even so, she hurled the arc-blade at Fate's back, but he was ready for it. Ducking down, dove inside the moving vehicle and slammed the door behind him.

Only that's not exactly what happened, no matter how it looked.

This was the real contingency: the lie he was trying to sell.

And on any other day I might have bought it, but not today. Today I was expecting tricks.

Tires squealing on the mosaic tiles of the plaza, the car roared away *without* him inside it.

I knew exactly what had happened. As he'd ducked inside the still moving car, he'd slapped at a button in the center of his chest and was gone. A short hop teleport lifted him out of the car even as it powered away, completing the illusion that his fifth man was getting him the fuck out of there while he materialized a couple of hundred meters away in the safety of the shadows around the side of the plaza. It was good. Better than good, actually. It was smart. That was unlike Fate. He would have got away with it if not for the fact that I had the surveillance camera on full zoom and, pixelated or not, even through the tinted windows of the black car, I could see every the subtle shift in the shadows of the interior that betrayed the fact that he wasn't sitting in the passenger seat as the car sped away.

The assassin chased the car out of the plaza, leaving her arc-blade where it had fallen.

I scanned the colonnades and vaults on either side of the plaza, high and low, looking for the telltale reflection from Fate's suit, for anything that might betray him, but he was already moving.

He couldn't hide from Mel Kamahi though. Her rig had already detected the new heat source his teleportation represented and locked onto it. He was running through a vectorized city on her screen, Mel watching him every step of the way as he picked a winding path through the canyons of super towers, trying to lose himself.

What that woman could do with a machine frightened me. She was easily the most dangerous of us all. She didn't need an arc-blade or hollow points to end a life. She was capable of far worse and didn't even have to leave her chair.

"Do you want me to bring him in?"

I shook my head. "No, let's just watch him, see if he makes contact. If he does, we've got him. If he doesn't, we have Imsen reach out. But for now, let him have his moment. I don't mind him thinking he's won this round."

I doubted myself long before Fate made contact.

I'm not arrogant enough to think I am infallible.

I freely admit that I don't know what goes on inside a man like Randall Fate's mind. I can try and guess. I can make assumptions, some even based on past experiences we've shared, but I can't ever *know*. So waiting for that call was hard. I expected him to try and fuck me. He had no reason to keep his promise. I certainly wasn't naïve enough to think he was an honorable man. But that only served to make him less predictable, not more so.

All I could do was wait.

I hate waiting.

I'm a man of action.

And, I'll be honest, I'm happiest when I'm fighting. That's my deepest darkest secret. My flaw. I am therefore I bleed. I bleed therefore I am. If I'm not bleeding, I'm not living. And no one wants to go through this life dead. That's just the way it is.

I did a trick with a coin rolling it across my knuckles first one way, then back again before making it disappear. It was a habit I'd picked up from Swann, I think. He was always doing it back when we first got together. It wasn't exactly high art, but the manual dexterity involved in it was good for close control, and for a little while it made me feel close to my old friend. In truth, it wasn't that much different from the old exercises Martagan used to do with her knife, but I was less likely to bleed if it went wrong. It took thirty seconds for one pass in one direction, a minute between flourishes. There's an element of insanity in doing the same thing over and over again. Say the same word often enough, and it will lose all meaning. Repeat the same action often enough, and it becomes part of your muscle memory. It's why we practice loading and reloading our weapons, stripping and rebuilding them, so we know each and every motion and can repeat them in pitch black conditions where our lives might just depend upon getting it right the first time, no fumbles.

The one thing I wasn't worried about was him not being able to find me.

On the fourth day, he came knocking.

It was a curt four-line message, each sentence truncated for maximum brevity. It came delivered inside the takeout boxes containing our food order:

Communication lines insecure. Make contact via the Dead Drop. You have twenty-four. No word I am out of here.

The dead drop.

I knew where he meant.

We'd used it back in the old days. Choosing it now was a homage to the past, surely? He was hoping I'd remember it, why it was significant to us, and think back on those days fondly.

He should have known better.

I don't have a sentimental bone in my body.

I approached the dead drop on foot.

I've painted a pretty picture of the world, I know. It's deceptive. Life isn't all towering glass super towers and too-bright neon lights, even if it isn't the air-cars vision of the future our ancestors had, it's a modern world, everything connected and interfaced and online and, well, for want of a better word, alive. But not *all* of it. Some stuff didn't fare so well in the transition to a corporation governed landscape. Of course, the rise of the corporations was brutal. We're not just talking espionage and dirty tricks, either. There are dead places, too. Places from before, places that suffered.

The dead drop is in the heart of a dead zone.

It's as if the outside world stops existing as you roll up to the Barrenlands.

You're no more than a hundred klicks from civilization, but you could easily imagine you were walking on the moon. As far as the eye can see there's nothing but irradiated earth and twisted metal, the occasional plinth of concrete with steel rebar poking out through the wounds in the stone like ribs exposed by the vicious slice of an arc-blade. It's an inhospitable landscape. It should be. After all, they dropped not one but two bombs on it to be sure nothing could ever grow back. Not the vegetation, not the population. Sometimes you forget about these dead zones that still litter the countryside, blinded by the bright, shiny towers of the cities. You forget that hundreds of thousands of people lived and died here. Of course, the corporations help us forget, too. Everything is bigger, brighter, better. They pump out slogans like 'Look to the Future!' and we swallow them whole. For people like us, those dead zones are a godsend, though.

Gant waited in the vehicle. I wanted to go in on foot. I didn't want to spook anyone.

It was brutally hot. Worse than Africa.

Beyond the plinths more broken walls slowly come into sight, covered with anti-war sentiment and ironic graffiti that is out of place with no real audience to appreciate it. The walls made up a place called The Labyrinth. Once upon a time, The Labyrinth had housed twenty-five thousand ordinary people with ordinary lives and ordinary hopes and dreams. Twenty-five thousand. Nowadays it feels like they cram that many into one of their damned Super Towers, but back then it had been an entire community. Now The Labyrinth houses the by-blows. Those poor souls spawned with the deformities of a radiation-fueled decade to fuck with their genetics. We're not talking third legs or second heads poking out of bellies or anything quite so grotesque, but I'm sure there's the odd third nipple and the like out there amid the blisters. Most of it is sickness and truncated lives, but there are slipped muscles and dropping faces that leave you with the impression that you're face-to-face with an imbecile. Of course, it just so happens to be an imbecile that'd gut you like a fish and chow down on your gonads for starters and fry your sweetmeats for dessert. Never underestimate the afflicted.

Where I needed to be was in the heart of The Labyrinth.

I moved quickly, but cautiously, listening for sounds that I was being followed. The by-blows would know I was in their territory. Nothing escaped their notice. It was just about getting out unmolested. I should have brought offerings. If I'd been more organized, I would have come bearing gifts—bits of burned out tech they could scavenge, circuits they could fuse and resistors they could bring stuttering back to life in some weird new form. They were wizards with dead technology. There wasn't anything they couldn't do—or at least it felt that way to the untrained eye. It was like stepping back a century in time to days when anything was possible, and nothing was regulated, the big corps nothing but a twinkle in the rich men's greedy eyes.

It didn't take long for me to hear them moving about around me, out of sight but definitely not out of mind. "Just passing through," I called. "No need to get excited. I'm not staying. I honor the treaty. I am not interested in your treasures, okay? I'm dropping off instructions at the dead drop, then moving on. Pass the message back to the elders, let them know I'm no threat."

I have no idea if it helped, but it never hurt to invoke the treaty—an accord that went back the best part of fifty years now, brokered by men like Fate who knew a good thing when they saw it. I heard some muttering followed by the sound of scampering feet, so the message was certainly being carried back to the den.

I scratched at my thumb.

I hadn't realized how hard I raked my other thumbnail across the skin until I drew blood. I knew what was going on. Withdrawal. It had been a long time since Fate had found me in the Beetle den. I wasn't quite climbing the walls, but there was no denying the hollowness inside me that was normally filled by that particular narcotic. And of course now I was thinking about it, I couldn't stop thinking about it.

I scratched harder. Not just my thumb this time, but halfway up the inside of my forearm, leaving angry red welts behind. I promised myself a few hours of blissful ignorance in a Beetle den before the final confrontation with Fate. I didn't want to go in half-assed, and to be honest, I was always at my best when I was climbing slowly down from a really good high. I don't know why. Maybe it's something to do with the chemical rush. Maybe it's all in my head, and I'm absolutely fucking useless and only think I'm like some golden god.

An engine roared in the distance. It didn't sound healthy. Was that Gant leaving? I hoped not. I didn't want to be faced with having to evac under fire without blazing chariot waiting to carry me out of hell.

I passed under a broken arch, entering The Labyrinth proper.

Across the way I saw two men walking, one leaning heavily on the other, head down, with the uneven gait of a slipped pelvis and bowed legs. Neither looked my way. Both were barefoot with skin like leather. I could smell them from a mile away. One raised a hand for me to follow. The elders had sent out guides. I did as I was told.

In territory like this, you're never off-guard. Let your defenses drop, you die. I knew why Fate had picked it. It wasn't just that it was remote, or that it was a wasteland, both strong factors in its favor, it was because of the by-blows. They provided an extra layer of protection. This way he didn't run the risk of being ambushed by me or anyone else. They wouldn't let us set up camp in their territory. There was no way to set up surveillance beyond a very grainy satellite image, and we could only manage that for as long as Mel Kamahi could get away with piggybacking a corporate feed, borrowing satellite time without being seen. It took time to recalibrate signals from the sky, too. The satellites needed to adjust their position and relay the signals back to earth. Meeting inside the city—any city—would have presented different challenges, but these dead zones were pretty much the last frontier in terms of the camera eye. They are watching you, make no mistake. Everywhere you go, every step you take, they're watching. The corporations collect and collate endless data about your everyday lives. Things you would think are pointless datapoints like what you ate for breakfast, how often you crap during a day, where you last fucked, and any and every addiction in between. These things all come together to help them predict the future, which is where they make their most money, by satisfying the needs you don't know you've even got yet. It's only a short leap to mind crimes and crap like that, where they know so much about you than can pinpoint intent before it's even formed in your mind. Fate used to say that neither side was honest, but it was the lies of the sledgehammer that upset him, not the lies of the peanut. I always took that to mean he could deal with the lies of our corporate paymasters because that was just their nature, but he couldn't cope with the lies we told one and other. There's a bitter irony in that, no? It's like saying how terrible the world is and just a small donation of ten dollars every month will make it a better place. If you're a sucker, you reach for your wallet every time. I was done with being a sucker. It wasn't my job to save the world.

I could feel Fate watching. He was in here.

They walked me through the shadows of the valley of death—a blisteringly hot expanse of wasteland in the center of The Labyrinth, so called because it was ground zero, the absolute nothing left behind by the bombs. This one had been a twofer, the first strike electromagnetic, the second with a thirty-two kiloton payload that cleared out a half-a-klick core. We walked into the epicenter of the bombs' five ring radius effect. At the core, everything had died. Everything. You could still taste the frisson in the air, the half-lives unleashed here still decaying and far from neutered. The second ring was no less terminal for mortal man but was designed primarily to take out automated machinery, wiping stuff like the banking networks to bring on chaos, while the third took out rail signaling and ignition systems. Beyond that, the fourth canceled out radio and television receivers, computer systems and mobile phones, while the fifth and final circle was battlefield tech, all of the support systems.

The dead drop was in one of the outer rings.

It had been an amusement park once upon a time, now it was like something out of the worst children's nightmare, with deformed clown-faces dripping down the front of derailed toy trains and the twisted bodies of legless unicorns on carousels. The centre of the carousel was an anchor-point of broken mirrors that offered up shards of the fun-fair in fractured horror where the silvering had blistered and left a pox of black spots on the glass that only served as a reminder of the melting flesh and screams that must have haunted this place on that last night of revelry as the nuclear wind burned the children and their parents to ash.

I'm not a religious man. I'm not a holy man. I don't believe in anything. Even so, I crossed myself as we walked through the rides toward what had been the old Tin Pan Alley with tin shooting galleries at the back.

My two guides watched me, the hunchback nodded encouragingly as I moved toward the silent stalls. It wasn't hard to imagine the barkers drumming up trade with promises of a prize every time and the metallic *pling* of the duck-shaped targets being shot down. I could almost smell the ghosts of cotton candy and saltwater taffy in the air.

The drop itself was inside the doors of the ghost train.

The faded faces of Dracula and Frankenstein looked out through curls of blistered paint whilst around them ghost hunters ran screaming from comical specters. None of the old carriages were on the rails. They lay overturned and wheelless on the wooden boards beside them.

I pushed through the doors and stepped through into darkness.

It was even hotter inside than it was outside.

Claustrophobically so.

The Day-Glo limbs of a plastic skeleton hanging by a rope were picked out momentarily as the sunlight streamed in through the double doors and vanished as they slammed closed again, leaving me alone in the dark. I could hear rats scratching around in the darkness. There's nothing more unnerving than an abandoned fun-fair, I don't care what anyone says, and I've been in some hellish places. But fun-fairs... they're meant to be full of life, vitality, screams and giggles and excitement, not like this. When they are left to rot like this, it's almost as though some emotional vampire had swooped down to suck all of the joy out of life, which, given Bela and Boris on the wall outside maybe wasn't so far off.

I stumbled forward, counting out eleven steps as I felt along the wall for the mechanism.

I resisted the temptation to call out to Fate.

My fingers found the switch. I pulled it. Somewhere deep inside the ghost train, old generators rumbled to life. I felt the vibrations through the old floorboards. There was a clank, and a clatter as the points on the metal rails shifted and the distant echo of one of the old cars rattling over them. I wasn't waiting for the car to sweep me off to some hidden vault, I needed the rails to move, that was all. With the points shifted it gave access to a flat panel of a false wall that just needed to be popped with a soft push to open and reveal the dead drop.

I had the time and the place already written on a piece of paper. I left it on the wooden table beside a box of matches so Fate could burn it and leave no trace of our communication. There were several small piles of black ash inside the room, testament to many such lost communiqués. Secrets were precious in this game, and a little paranoia never hurt anyone.

I checked the room for anything Fate might have left for me to find, but the place was bare. Was this where he'd sold us out? It was a chilling thought. More chilling was the fact that one of those piles of ash probably signified the death sentences passed on Martagan and Swann.

Well, it would be over soon.

I backed out of the room and killed the power to the rails. The sound of the junction dropping back into place echoed through the darkness. The light was only fifteen steps away, but it had never felt so far away.

He was late.

I began to think he wouldn't show.

And when that thought took root, it festered.

The more it festered, the more I began to suspect I'd opened myself up to a world of hurt. There was no getting away from the fact he had proven himself a treacherous bastard. Yes, he'd let me pick the time and the place, but that didn't mean much in the scheme of things. It certainly wasn't a guarantee of safety. He'd had more than enough time since I'd left the message in the dead drop to set a trap if that's what he intended, even if I'd tried to be clever in my choice of locations.

I'd given him six hours to get in place. The meet was two hours from the dead drop. I hoped he appreciated my choice. Climbing the stairs to the top of the Wan Chai plaza super tower, eighty-six stories above Old Tokyo, surrounded on all sides by the familiar views of the city set against a backdrop of stars. The neon was a thing of beauty. It all bled together in streaks with the rain coming down.

I walked out to the middle of the rooftop. It was a vast expanse. There was no way you'd accidentally stumble and tumble off the edge, given the edge was more than four hundred meters away from the roof access. Gant was across the plaza, hidden behind the stained glass of the Sky Church's chapel. I knew he was watching through the scope of his Predator KVK. Called upon, he wouldn't miss. Gant's aim was dead-eye. Even with the combination of the wind, rain, and distance, I knew I could trust him. Of course, his bullets were just my back up. I had no intention of shooting first.

But Fate was pissing me off big time.

I'd gone out of my way to make him feel at home when I ruined what was left of his life, right down to the choice of location. He only needed to turn up. And that just meant riding the express elevator to the top of his own building and taking a couple of flights of stairs to the roof. It wasn't like I'd asked him to trek across the Sahara. But he still wasn't here, and the clock was ticking.

"Do we have eyes on the mark?" I said, my voice picked up by the micro-transmitter woven into the fabric of my shirt collar.

"Negative," Mel Kamahi said. "Fate hasn't entered the building."

We were all in place.

The wind buffeted me while the rain plastered my hair flat to my scalp. I didn't move. I didn't turn my back from the view. The reason was the black speck I'd noticed on the horizon, moving low but fast across the rooftops. It was a Viper—an attack helo. We're talking one seriously armed piece of kit, security forces grade, a mobile war machine. You didn't see them over the cities unless there was a riot to quell. The streets were as peaceful as I'd ever seen them, which meant the Viper had another reason for being here, like, delivering Randall Fate to the rooftop meet. I followed the helo blades as they chopped through the deluge. Its high-intensity searchlight picked me out. It was blindingly bright. I still didn't move.

Down below, life went on oblivious.

I raised my head to stare right into the blinding white lights without shielding my eyes. It was a dumb move. Bravado. I didn't want Fate to think he had me at a disadvantage. I can be a prick like that, even when it costs me to do it.

Bring it on, *Fate*, I thought grimly, waiting for the helo slowly circling the plaza.

If he'd been smart Fate would have had the searchlight sweep the entire plaza, but he was intent on staring me down. I'm not sure if that meant he knew there was no threat to his life, or if he was absolutely preoccupied with me. I'd like to think it was the latter. Nothing wrong with having a bit of an ego in this game. After all, I was very much alive and well despite multiple attempts to put an end to that.

Mel's voice crackled into life in my ear. "He's here." I almost said, "No shit," but realized the Viper wouldn't be showing up on her screens, so Fate had walked in through the front door whilst I was staring up at the helo. I was beginning to work out how he thought. The presence of the Viper circling the plaza was no coincidence. Just like the black car before, it would be part of his exit strategy, but this time the short-hop teleport would be rigged to pluck him off the rooftop and put him squarely in the helo's passenger seat so the pilot could make like a shepherd and get him the fuck out of there if things went south. It was a good plan save for one small thing Fate had overlooked.

Tenebrae.

She was my wild card.

I heard the access door open.

"You took your time," I said, still not turning around. This was an important moment in my life. It's pretty rare that you know you're in the middle of an iconic moment at the time, but there was no doubting just how big this one was. We're talking student and teacher facing each other one last time, the tables turning as the student finally becomes the master.

"Things are a bit," Fate seemed to struggle to find the word he wanted to use. He settled on, "complicated."

"I'm sure they are."

"I'm in trouble, Marco. I've made some mistakes. I don't have anyone to turn to."

"I know how that feels."

"I don't think you do," he said, full of self-pity. "I thought I saw a way out. Instead, I think I opened the door to hell."

"That's a bit fucking melodramatic, man," I said, enjoying the moment. "Do you have the drive?"

I heard his wet footsteps as he moved across the rooftop toward me.

"It's safe," he said.

"But it's not here," I finished for him. "How did I know you'd try and dick me around at the last moment, Fate? You just can't help yourself, can you?"

"It's not like that," he said. But that, of course, was exactly what it was like. We both knew it. He couldn't resist trying to renegotiate the terms of our agreement. It was just the way he was, like the scorpion that stings the turtle, so the pair of them drown together. It's just his nature. And that, of course, was what I'd been banking on.

"So what is it like, my old friend," I said, laying it on a bit thick, I'll admit. "Tell me. I picked this place for privacy so we can talk openly without fear of being overheard. I assume you've swept the place to confirm that fact we're alone?"

"Of course," Fate said. I believed him. He was just paranoid enough to think everyone was out to get him. Of course, the only person who was really gunning for him just happened to be the one person he had turned to for help. Now that, my friends, is ironic.

"So this mistake? All I want is the drive you promised me, the rest is just crap I need to get through to get it, so don't make me drag it out of you."

"I don't want to talk to your back, Marco. I want to see your face."

I turned around slowly, tears of rain running down my scarred cheeks.

"Talk to me."

"I made myself dispensable. It was a stupid thing to do. I thought it was a way out. A quick score. A way to get some cash and just disappear and be done with this life. I don't have the heart for it anymore, Marco. I'm getting old. I want to have a yacht in the Bahamas and soak up the sun until I get skin cancer and shrivel up like Tutankhamen's balls."

"What did you do?"

"I sold them my brain."

"You did *what*?"

"I let them pattern it. I don't know how the fuck it works, you know me and technology, but they hooked me up to a machine in some fancy lab and dumped all of my memories and instincts onto a server. I didn't realize who was behind it. I thought it was a good deal. Fuck, I didn't actually think it'd work. But they can use what they downloaded to overwrite some poor slob's brain and turn him into me. And not just once. You saw what Akachi were doing back there, we're talking a fucking clone army."

"And for that, they want to kill you? Surely they'd want to kiss your feet?"

"They don't need me anymore," Fate said.

"Okay, so what's this got to do with me?"

"I need you to help me."

I let the plea hang between us for a second, drawing the silence out, before I said, "I don't think so."

"You want that drive, you need to protect me, Marco. If I die, your chance of getting your hands on it dies with me. So you need to ask yourself how much do you want what's on that drive?"

Little did he know, of course. I was so tempted to tell him there and then I didn't give a shit about the drive, but that would have defeated the whole point of the con. He'd bought the hurrah. I was in absolute control here. Time for the In-and-In, the glorious endgame. I could no more back out now than he could. This was when I had to throw my hand in with Fate. Of course, in this case, it wasn't about cash. I needed to invest something different in the con. Me.

"I want it," I lied. I felt like an actress in some sleazy porno really, telling the lead just how badly she wanted him whilst staring up dumbly at the camera, wishing she was anywhere else but there.

"Then help me disappear. I need a new life."

"Are you really sure they're out to get you?" I said. I knew my voice was being picked up by the hidden mic and carrying to the rest of my crew. We'd agreed on an audio cue. All I had to say was "I'm in." And Tenebrae would make damn sure we sold just how 'in' I was to Fate.

"I don't know, Randall," I said. "If things are as fucked as you say, they'll know who I am, and going up against them will paint a big red target on my back. There's no going back from that."

"I've got money," Fate said. "I can make it worth your while."

"If that were true, we wouldn't be here now."

"Fuck you, man. Don't make me beg."

The Viper moved around behind the Super Tower, still circling, it's searchlight still lighting every corner and angle of the rooftop.

"Help me, and I'll help you. You get what you want," Fate pleaded. "You get the info that'll bring the corp down. You get to be the idealist. You'll be a fucking legend, my friend. Everything we've ever done, every sucker deal we've ever bled for, you'll make it all worthwhile. You'll own them. That's the only language these corporations understand. You'll have the power."

"Okay," I said, making sure the next two words carried through the rain to where the assassin was ready to do her thing. "I'm in."

I heard a whistle, out of place in the buzz above the city. It cut through the drumming of the rain on the steel and glass structure. Fate heard it, too. He turned, following the sound with his gaze, in time to catch the rocket's red glare the instant before the Type III shell from the M76 rocket launcher tore into the armored side of the helo. In the silence between heartbeats nothing happened, and then as another 70 ml of blood was pumped through our systems, the searchlight died, throwing us into momentary darkness before shell exploded, ripping the helo apart from the inside out. Twisted metal spun away, the core of the fireball blazing white-hot as it lit the sky, turning night briefly to day. The wreckage rained down on the unsuspecting pedestrians in Wan Chen plaza. We were too high to hear the screams.

Fate stared at the fireball that had been his escape route. Behind the blazing helo, reflections in the stained glass of the Sky Church danced insanely, a thousand devils tearing it up merrily. Behind the glass, Gant would be counting down the seconds until his first shot.

That single shot would ram home the implications of what was happening: they'd found him.

That one shot would give Fate rope burns as the noose tightened around his neck.

The best part of it was that the bastard was still blissfully ignorant of the fact that mine were the hands doing the strangling.

The helo hung in the sky for a second longer, then scattered, showering blazing wreckage across the plaza below and plunging us into darkness.

"They must have followed you! You stupid fuck. Didn't you think they'd be tailing you? Fuck. Just... fuck. We need to move," I barked, grabbing his hand and pulling him toward the access door. My panic sold my innocence. The In-and-In.

Fate ran for the door.

Fate was mine.

He ducked through the door as Gant's first bullet tore into the cement around the frame. The shot was so close it was hard to believe it wasn't meant to kill him. Gant was either very good or very lucky. The huge steel door slammed behind us, echoing with the impact of another bullet. The stairwell was five degrees colder than the night outside. We ran down the concrete stairs two and three at a time, the handrail the only thing that stopped us from an uncontrolled descent. Fate didn't look back once to see if I was following. Self-preservation is a fierce instinct.

Before we were down the second flight of stairs, doubling back on ourselves, I shouted, "Your place."

"We can't go back there, that's exactly what they'll expect," he objected. "What about your team? Are they in place?"

"They are, but they won't be much help if Bleeders come

storming up the stairs. We need weapons. You've got a fucking arsenal in there. We're tooling up before we set foot outside. The damn place is a fortress."

He tried to argue, but with me chasing him down the stairwell it was a fight he wasn't going to win.

Mel had the service elevator waiting for us. The door opened as Fate slammed his hand against the call button. We rushed in. The steel cage messed with our communications set-up. Once the doors closed, we'd be out of earshot with Mel and the rest of the crew. Radio silence is unnerving in this game. It just is. Communication is everything. Before Fate could press the button for the lobby, I hit the one for his floor. He looked at me. "Don't take this the wrong way, but if I'm putting my life on the line for you, I want pay."

For a second he didn't know what to say. Then he tried, "I'll see you right."

"No offense, but I don't trust you."

"I don't carry any cash, you know that."

"There's a computer in your place. While I'm grabbing the guns and ammo, make a deposit into my work account. You've got the details. You want to hire me to protect you, then you pay for the privilege like anyone else would."

He nodded as if it made perfect sense. You get what you pay for is a fairly common truism in our game. "How much?"

"You know what I cost," I said. Everyone has got their price.

The doors opened, and we were back online.

I followed Fate into his place. He didn't turn the light on as we entered. Even knowing that those huge plate glass windows that offered that incredible panorama of Old Tokyo were reinforced and absolutely bulletproof, he didn't want any watchers to know we were in there. I went straight for the arsenal, carefully selecting my weapon of choice. I grabbed something for Fate and went back through to the lounge where he had the terminal switched on and was in the process of triggering a million dollar transaction from his offshore account to mine. Looking at the zeroes on the screen it was chump change to him. I began to realize just how much he'd skimmed off the top of our fifty gigs over the years as management fees before he'd paid the rest of us our cut. It was all about money. I also knew this wasn't even the half of it. Fate had a desert island account. He used to joke about it being his pension. There were other assets too.

As far as I could tell he hadn't set foot in here since my last visit. The fugu takeaway box was still on the counter where I'd fished it out of the trash.

In my ear, Mel said, "Okay, got everything, account number, password, the only thing I need now is for him to trigger the actual payment and we've got access to every cent he has."

"Good to go?" I asked Fate. He looked up. I watched his fingers. His pinky was resting on the return key, but he hadn't pushed it and until he did that money was going nowhere. It was only one account though. It didn't touch his desert island funds or any of those intangible assets I knew he'd stashed. But he'd been telling the truth, that last job had made him richer than god. Thankfully he'd left the lion's share in the job account which we were about to clean out, and there wasn't a thing he could do about it—apart from not press the return key and keep Mel locked out. He hesitated a second more, then hit return.

"Got it," Mel said, triumphantly.

I moved up to stand behind Fate, looking over his shoulder. Instinctively, he shut the screen down, protective of his secrets. I put a finger to the earpiece in my right ear, as if I were getting an incoming communiqué. "They've breached the building, Fate. Mel's counting three teams coming in from below and she's got eyes on for a helo coming in fast from the East." I picked the direction carefully. It was the only one you didn't have a view of from the apartment windows. "You know how this is going to have to go down," I said, doing my best to sound reasonable. "We can hole up here for a week, I can protect you, my team is almost as good as we were, but there's no way we're getting you out of this building alive." I deliberately didn't look at the takeaway carton on the counter, I wanted him to come up with that idea all by himself, I just planted the thought in his mind subliminally. The power of suggestion is one scary fucking thing. "And shit, look, let's be brutally honest, even if we get you out of here, you can never be you again, right, you get that? Randall Fate is dead. That means all of those accounts, all of those hidden assets, the desert island account, the lot, gone. You won't be able to touch them because the moment you do it'll bring a world of corporate hurt down on you."

"What the fuck do we do? What the fuck do we do? Jesus..." it was like a mantra, it made no sense, he just kept repeating the words over and over again as if they would suddenly crystallize into a plan.

"I don't know," I said, then paused, seeming to have this off the wall idea.

He looked at me filled with hope. "What? What is it?"

"There's an assassin on my team. Her broker... he knows people. He's kept her identity hidden for years, working as a go-between. We could approach him... maybe he could hide you the same way?"

"That's good. Yeah. That's good. That could work."

"It won't be cheap," I said.

"Fuck the money. I've got money. What I don't have is nine lives."

Even if he did, by my reckoning he'd used up all of them anyway.

"Even so, you won't be able to touch your funds, they'll be monitoring your accounts, waiting for you to touch the money. The minute you do, hammer time."

"There's got to be a way we can work around that?" Fate sounded desperate now, reading to jump at any lifeline I offered him. What else could I do?

"Let me check something," I said, then pressed my finger to the earbud again as if instigating communication. "Mel, how difficult would it be for you to create a new identity, top to bottom, nothing that could trace back to Fate or us?" I paused a beat, the identity and accounts were all in place, he just needed to think this was a mercy dash not a red-hot poker up the financial ass. "Uh huh, yeah, right, uh huh." Lots of positive sounds. I gave Fate the thumbs up. "We don't need all the papers yet, obviously, but we need to set that stuff in motion, and it needs to be legit, or as close to so it stands up to scrutiny. Uh huh, yeah. If you can set it up for new prints, corneal transplant, et cetera, I'll worry about getting him to the docs. We're going to need somewhere to dump his assets though, and it can't be a straight transfer, these guys aren't stupid. We'll need to liquidize everything, then shift it through a dozen factors rinsing it until no one has a clue where it came from. Great, look, I'll leave that with you. We've got bigger fish to fry right now. The enemy's at the door."

This particular enemy would come dressed as Tenebrae in just a couple of minutes, so we had to work fast to push Fate over the edge.

Fate snapped the chain that hung around his neck and handed me the small pendant that had hung on it.

"Everything you need is on there." He looked nervously toward the door. He was every bit as fidgety as any Beetle addict I'd ever seen. He knew what was coming up those stairs, and just how impossible it'd be for the two of us to fight them off. "Give it to your geek, she'll be able to crack the encryption and make sense of stuff. It's fairly straightforward. I'm trusting you, Marco." He kept saying that, trying to reinforce the message in my brain. I understood the psychology of it. It wouldn't work this time. "Everything I have, everything I am, is on that. Without it, I'm nothing."

"You can trust me," I said as I pocketed it, then reached up to touch the earbud again, and broke into a fake conversation with Mel, reporting back, "They've got twelve men on the stairwells and the elevators are down. We can't go to the roof, the helo will be in place before we are. We're between the Devil and the deep blue sea, mate. Is there another way out of here? A bolt hole you haven't told us about?"

Fate shook his head.

"Okay, I need to think. Take this," I handed him the gun I'd picked up in the armory. "Anything comes through that door, shoot it."

He laughed at that. "This isn't my first time at the rodeo, big guy."

"All I care about is that it isn't your last." That shut him up.

I moved across the work surface in the kitchen area, my hand resting on the counter inches from the festering scraps of fugu. "The only way we're getting you out of here is in a box," I said. Two could play at those subliminal games.

Someone hammered on the other side of the door, the butt of a gun resounding off the steel.

Fate squeezed off a round, the shells ripping into the six-inch thick security door. Even hollow-points couldn't punch clean through the steel. The impacts resonated through the glass and steel structure in a tortuous chorus.

The hammering came again.

"How long with the door hold?" I asked Fate.

"Depends what they've brought to open it, and just how determined they are to get through."

"Best guess?"

"Not long enough."

"We need to be clever. I'm not ready for some foolish grand last stand. There's got to be a way of getting you out of here."

"You said it yourself, the only way I'm getting out of here is in a box."

"Like GenX," I said, and there it was, out there. He'd left one impossible situation seemingly dead. All we had to do was replicate those circumstances.

He looked at the takeaway carton beside me, and a light came on. "We can do that. Exactly that. Oh yes, that's fucking brilliant. You're a genius, Marco. You're a cold stone genius. Do everything I say, and we might just get out of this."

"Okay," I said, dubiously. "What are you thinking?"

The hammering intensified on the door, then followed by a dull clang. C4 being attached to the frame. We didn't have long until Tenebrae blew the door off its hinges. "Go get a blade from the armory, I'll sort stuff out here."

I heard him rattle around in the cutlery drawer, and then scrape around the contents of the takeaway carton, scratching up whatever poison remained. When I returned, he'd got enough Tetrodotoxin to down an elephant. "Give me the blade." I handed it over. Fate smeared poison across the surface of the blade. "When they come in, I need you to stab me."

I shook my head. "Kinda defeats the point, doesn't it?"

"Avoid the vital organs and major arteries. Just get it in somewhere nice and soft, and the toxins on the blade will do the rest. Don't do any damage that can't be fixed. Make like you're using me as a human shield. Make sure they see the knife go in. Give it five seconds or so, and the toxins will slow my heart to the point the beat is negligible, nearly two minutes between each. I'll register dead on every monitor they hook me up to. Then you just walk out of there. Either they leave me behind, and you come back to get me, or they take me out of there in a box, and you bust me out and revive me when it's safe."

"You think this is going to work?"

"They want me dead. Let's give them what they want."

With pleasure, I thought.

I moved to stand behind Fate, wrapping my left arm around his neck and resting the fugu-poisoned arc-blade against his ribs.

We waited for the door to open and Tenebrae to stride through.

I counted down the seconds. The timer the assassin had affixed to the explosives joined in the countdown with ten seconds to go before the explosion tore the door from its hinges and warped the frame, leaving behind a ragged hole where the six-inch thick steel had stood between us. She stepped through the ruined doorway, a cold smile on her face. Dirt and dust smeared her ebony skin. "You're a hard man to kill, Randall Fate," she said. "But then I should have known you would be," she tapped her temple knowingly.

I tightened my grip on his throat. "Stay where you are," I said.

"I'm not interested in you," she cocked her head to one side, as if trying to remember where she'd seen me before. Her smile parted slightly. "Marco. You can walk away from this. I'm only interested in Fate. Don't make this your problem."

"How much will you give me for him?" I asked.

"No bargains. No bartering. No deals. I'm here to kill him."

"I can do that for you," I said, and with a single swift slice, opened Fate's side. Blood spilled over my fingers as it stained his shirt. Fate howled in pain, clutching at his side as if to try and stem the flow of blood even as it thickened to the point the material could no longer soak it up and leaked through his fingers.

"I don't care how he dies," the assassin says, I get paid if it's your blade or mine that does the killing."

"In that case, would you mind terribly if I gut the fucker? He killed two of my best friends."

"Ah, yes," the assassin said, seemingly dredging Fate's memory up. "Swann and Martagan. Yes. Did he tell you why he betrayed them?"

I shook my head.

"Greed," she said, matter-of-factly.

"Is that true, Fate? It was all about the money?"

I felt him nod, his hair brushing against my cheek.

"I hope you rot in hell you bastard," and whispered in his ear, and rammed the knife home, twisting it so that it *hurt*.

He collapsed in my arms, heart beating erratically. I counted to five in my head, then checked his neck for a pulse. I looked up at the assassin. "He's gone. Time to get him out of here. Mel, can you hear me?"

"Loud and clear, boss."

"I've got some sort of pendant, looks like it's hardcoded with all of his secrets. I'll need you to crack that before we wake him up."

"Gotcha."

"Gant, you out there?"

The big man came into the room carrying a metal coffin.

Time to have some fun.

We didn't wake him for a week.

We had to get our ducks in a row first.

Most importantly, we needed to move his body back to Africa.

Imsen made arrangements for the transport. I admit part of me would have been happy to just put him in the ground and let him wake up and linger for a couple of days before the air ran out. But that really wouldn't have been a fate worse than death. I wanted to do what I'd promised from the start, so I contacted Research and Development at Akachi and put the wheels in motion.

At first, I wasn't sure they could do what I wanted, and then I wasn't sure they would do it.

Some people have a strong sense of morality. I needed a scientist who was more driven by curiosity than bounded by ethics. I found one, finally. I knew I would. It was only ever going to be a matter of time. The pendant helped. He'd been telling the truth when he said that pendent contained everything he was. It was all on there. His entire life of fighting and bleeding was written there, just waiting to be extrapolated from a history of violence that curdled the blood.

He was a bad man. A very bad man.

The stone contained a silica-based Micro-drive, capable of storing vast quantities of data even if it looked no more exciting than a little geode on a gold chain.

It took her a couple of days, but Mel Kamahi unearthed every single one of his secrets. We're talking way beyond just money and ferreted away assets here. We're talking enemy lists. Everyone who wanted him dead, every grudge he'd racked up, every man he'd ever crossed, we're talking gold dust. People, in other words, with an interest in making Randall Fate hurt. Including a man who was only too happy to help us break Fate. Mel explained the concept to him in as simple terms as possible: "It's a bit like flatlining. You leave him inside the machine, but there's no way back to his body." The concept delighted our doc.

"A prison of the mind?"

"Exactly."

It's amazing quite how much information you can store on a machine.

But that's technology, isn't it? A perpetual quest to make the world simultaneously smaller on the outside while vastly bigger on the inside.

We delivered the body by hand, Mel helping in the procedure every step of the way.

We could have walked away at that point, there was nothing else we needed to do. It was job done. But I wanted to be there when he woke up.

I wanted my face to be the first one he saw.

I wanted, for just a second, him to experience a rush of hope.

And then I wanted to break him.

I looked around the room. The team were in place, surgical masks over their mouths, they were a cluster of eyes, no more, no less. Tenebrae, Mel Kamahi and Rowell Gant. My team. My family. The machinery was primed. All that remained was to turn it on and wake Fate. End it finally, and begin it all over again.

I looked at the doc. He nodded. The rest of his team confirmed their readiness.

They ran through their startup routine. They were good at their job. Fate's body had already been incinerated. I'd toyed with the idea of purging his mind and leaving his empty body to taunt him but decided against it. It wasn't that it was cruel and unusual, or that dangling the carrot of hope could backfire against me if he found a way to escape the machine. None of that really factored into my decision in the end. I just wanted to watch him burn.

I'd poured the gasoline on the pyre myself, and warmed my hands on the flames as his flesh was reduced to ash.

All that remained of my old mentor was structures and subroutines on the machine now.

Funny to think that what had started as a con became the foundation for my revenge. But I guess that's the thing with science. Someone has to imagine it, then someone else can make it happen. The quest for immortality is as old as the hills. Everyone is obsessed with living forever. Well, everyone except for us Bleeders. We know better. We know that death is a release.

Immortality is most definitely a fate worse than death.

I said, "Let's get this party started."

The doc moved down the line of glossy screens, triggering commands until Fate 2.0 came online.

His face slowly reconstructed itself in the center of the main screen.

Froze in place.

Tried to speak, but couldn't. Tried to move, but couldn't. There was a camera above the screen. I stared into its black lens, giving the facial recognition software time to map my features, then turned my attention to the screen beneath it.

I watched the panic set in.

It knew me. He was in there. It had worked. The horror of it made me realize what kind of hell I must have put Mel through when I'd kept her trapped in that flatline right at the beginning of this revenge trip. I owed her. Big time.

"Can you hear me, Fate?" I asked, speaking slowly, clearly. "Look around you, I'll give you a moment. It would have been too easy to kill you. Plus, I'd given you my word. That means something to me. I'm a man of principle. My word is my bond. It's about honor. You wouldn't understand that. There's no way you are going to die on my watch. You've paid for my services. You've paid a lot of money for them, in fact. Everything you ever had. I want you to consider yourself protected. Forever. Well, not forever, for as long as there's air in my lungs and blood pumping through my veins. A long time. I don't intend to die until I am very old. I just came into something of a windfall. I've got my eye on a little desert island somewhere warm to settle down and retire. I should warn you, I've been talking to the doc a lot over the last week, while you've been gone. He reckons you'll experience phantom pains for years to come, they'll be quite real, I'm told. You'll be trying to move hands that aren't there, trying to scratch itches that are only in your head. Thoughts that before came tumbling through your head will process so quickly now you'll have the answers before you've finished consciously forming them, second-guessing yourself all the time. No doubt you'll slowly go mad. That's an understandable side effect of this new life of yours. But before then, you're going to have a long time to think about what happened, about what you did to Swann and Martagan. About how you betrayed them. They didn't deserve to die. Not like that. They trusted you. You betrayed their trust. You deserve this. I burned your body myself. It's important you know that. There's no going back. I watched it sear and char and blister and finally collapse in on itself, all of the juices cooked out of it. This is your life now, Fate. This is all there is. Think about it. Process it."

Sensors reported the kernel panic at its core as it understood it had no mouth, no body. All that remained were thought processes that might laughingly have been called his soul.

One by one the servers and systems attached to the machine started to make the most hideous sounds, grinding, grating, overloading.

It took me a moment to realize that the machine was screaming.

"I win," I said, and walked away.

FROM THE PUBLISHER

Thank you for reading *One Man's War*.

We hope you enjoyed it as much as we enjoyed bringing it to you. We just wanted to take a moment to encourage you to review the book on Amazon and Goodreads. Every review helps further the author's reach and, ultimately, helps them continue writing fantastic books for us all to enjoy.

If you liked *One Man's War*, check out the rest of our catalogue at www.aethonbooks.com. To sign up to receive a FREE collection from some of our best authors as well as updates regarding all new releases, visit www.subscribepage.com/AethonReadersGroup.

SPECIAL THANKS TO:

ADAWIA E. ASAD
JENNY AVERY
BARDE PRESS
CALUM BEAULIEU
BEN
BECKY BEWERSDORF
BHAM
TANNER BLOTTER
ALFRED JOSEPH BOHNE IV
CHAD BOWDEN
ERREL BRAUDE
DAMIEN BROUSSARD
CATHERINE BULLINER
JUSTIN BURGESS
MATT BURNS
BERNIE CINKOSKE
MARTIN COOK
ALISTAIR DILWORTH
JAN DRAKE
BRET DULEY
RAY DUNN
ROB EDWARDS
RICHARD EYRES
MARK FERNANDEZ
CHARLES T FINCHER
SYLVIA FOIL
GAZELLE OF CAERBANNOG
DAVID GEARY
MICHEAL GREEN
BRIAN GRIFFIN
EDDIE HALLAHAN
JOSH HAYES
PAT HAYES
BILL HENDERSON
JEFF HOFFMAN
GODFREY HUEN
JOAN QUERALTÓ IBÁÑEZ
JONATHAN JOHNSON
MARCEL DE JONG
KABRINA
PETRI KANERVA
ROBERT KARALASH
VIKTOR KASPERSSON
TESLAN KIERINHAWK
ALEXANDER KIMBALL
JIM KOSMICKI
FRANKLIN KUZENSKI
MEENAZ LODHI
DAVID MACFARLANE
JAMIE MCFARLANE
HENRY MARIN
CRAIG MARTELLE
THOMAS MARTIN
ALAN D. MCDONALD
JAMES MCGLINCHEY
MICHAEL MCMURRAY
CHRISTIAN MEYER
SEBASTIAN MÜLLER
MARK NEWMAN
JULIAN NORTH
KYLE OATHOUT
LILY OMIDI
TROY OSGOOD
GEOFF PARKER
NICHOLAS (BUZ) PENNEY
JASON PENNOCK
THOMAS PETSCHAUER
JENNIFER PRIESTER
RHEL
JODY ROBERTS
JOHN BEAR ROSS
DONNA SANDERS
FABIAN SARAVIA
TERRY SCHOTT
SCOTT
ALLEN SIMMONS
KEVIN MICHAEL STEPHENS
MICHAEL J. SULLIVAN
PAUL SUMMERHAYES
JOHN TREADWELL
CHRISTOPHER J. VALIN
PHILIP VAN ITALLIE
JAAP VAN POELGEEST
FRANCK VAQUIER
VORTEX
DAVID WALTERS JR
MIKE A. WEBER
PAMELA WICKERT
JON WOODALL
BRUCE YOUNG

www.ingramcontent.com/pod-product-compliance
Lightning Source LLC
Chambersburg PA
CBHW030413310726
48979CB00002B/402

* 9 7 8 1 9 4 9 8 9 0 4 7 1 *